Never Miss Your Best Friend

Author of *Just Friends* and *A Lot Like Love…A Li'l Like Chocolate,* twenty-two-year-old Sumrit Shahi is one of the youngest bestselling authors in the country. He is also the screenwriter for the popular shows, *Sadda Haq* and *Million Dollar Girl,* on Channel V. When he's not writing bestsellers or trying to make TV serials cooler, he attends a bartending course. He's also taken a certified course (yes, there is one) in UFO studies. An MUN-er and national-level debater, he's a graduate in Liberal Arts from Symbiosis International University, Pune. Sumrit is currently based in Mumbai where he doesn't get as awesome rajma chawal as in his hometown, Chandigarh.

To find out what Sumrit's up to next, follow him on Facebook: https://www.facebook.com/sumrit.shahi

Never Kiss Your Best Friend

Sumrit Shahi

RUPA

Published by
Rupa Publications India Pvt. Ltd 2015
7/16, Ansari Road, Daryaganj
New Delhi 110002

Sales centres:
Allahabad Bengaluru Chennai
Hyderabad Jaipur Kathmandu
Kolkata Mumbai

Copyright © Sumrit Shahi 2015

This is a work of fiction. Names, characters, places and incidents are either the product of the author's imagination or are used fictitiously, and any resemblance to any actual persons, living or dead, events or locales is entirely coincidental.

All rights reserved.
No part of this publication may be reproduced, transmitted, or stored in a retrieval system, in any form or by any means, electronic, mechanical, photocopying, recording or otherwise, without the prior permission of the publisher.

ISBN: 978-81-291-3485-1

Second impression 2015

10 9 8 7 6 5 4 3 2

The moral right of the author has been asserted.

Typeset by SÜRYA, New Delhi

Printed at Thomson Press, India Ltd, Faridabad

This book is sold subject to the condition that it shall not, by way of trade or otherwise, be lent, resold, hired out, or otherwise circulated, without the publisher's prior consent, in any form of binding or cover other than that in which it is published.

Indebted to His Holiness, Satguru Babaji Hardev Singh Ji Maharaj, for teaching me that God is formless (Nirankar) and you can find him in the person sitting next to you.

Dedicated to the three most important women in my life: Mrs Inderjeet Kholi (my grandmom), Mrs Smiley Shahi (my mom) and Rabbani (my angel).

Ek tuhi Nirankar
Mein teri sharan han
Mainu baksh lo

Contents

Prologue 1

Part 1: Lived. Liked. Loved. Lost. And then I met him again. 3

Part 2: Lived. Liked. Loved. And then I lost him. 27

Part 3: Regret. And a few choices. 177

Epilogue 203

Acknowledgements 205

Prologue

Listen life,
I've had pancakes without maple syrup.
I've been constipated on long journeys.
I've stayed at home and finished shitty assignments on a Saturday night.
I've walked in on my parents while they have been at it.
I've had my tongue stuck in someone's braces.
I've lost biscuits to hot chai.
I've sat hungover through early morning lectures at college.
I've unsuccessfully hidden hickeys from my father.
I've made peace with my Al-Qaeda picture on my driving licence.
I've lost my ATM card more than once.
I've been served Pepsi when I've asked for Coke and not made a fuss about it.
Hell! I've even been sober in Goa for an entire trip.
So when my flatmate-cum-colleague, Shruti, announced at breakfast, then appealed again at lunch and finally pleaded during dinner that it's a Saturday night and we must go out clubbing and live a little, and I agreed, all I was asking of you was a harmless night of some self-gratifying attention, probably a little cardio on the dance floor and that much-needed drunk action that I could happily regret the next morning over lime water and a strip of aspirin in my bed; or even better—someone else's.

Someone with a cute butt, sculpted muscles and some brains. That's just about it.

Life, in the end I am just another single twenty-five-year-old girl, alone and somewhat lonely in a big city, who talks to Siri on her iPhone 8 when she is bored, who obviously feels her job doesn't pay her enough, the right guys don't notice her enough and her parents don't love her enough, otherwise why would they want her to be courted by Chaddha Uncle's son who loves his 'Lyuee-Vithan' belts more than a civilized conversation, every time she is forced to meet him back at home in Chandigarh?

Life, it's high time we fell for each other. I did not disown you when you dispelled my teenage belief in actually falling in love before making it. I hung onto you even as I ventured on the journey of what is conventionally called 'growing up'. I did not desert you even as you made me navigate a road of not-my-type boys, making me halt mostly at the wrong relationships, conveniently speeding past old friendships and old joys.

Life, I know you've got a raging boner all the time and mostly you don't carry lubricant. I've accepted my position in our little arrangement.

So. Why? Why? Why?
Why did you have to do this?
Why did you make me meet HIM?
All over again?

Yours, till I die. Or you kill me. Either way.

Tanie

Part 1

Lived. Liked. Loved. Lost.
And then I met him again.

17 April 2020
10.15 p.m.

'Damn!' I said in the same instant I got up from my bed.

The stilettos stung.

Coaxing my feet to endure a night of torture and some unhealthy bondage, I managed a soldier walk to the mirror and quickly took a final, last-minute customary glance at myself.

The fair skin with traces of permeated pollution and tan. The wavy shoulder-length hair, tired of experimentation and changing colours. The petite five-foot-three-inch frame, standing tall on a makeshift world of plastic and glass. The kohl-lined eyes, weary yet longing. The glossed lips, parched with all the smoking. The faint traces of cellulite on the triceps. The rajma-chawal genetics. The foetus of a beer belly. Yet a clever dress, which accentuated the cuts, hugged the miniscule curves and revealed what didn't need to be concealed.

I walked out to Shruti's room and knocked on the door. Politely.

'Shruti. I'm ready.'

'Go fuck yourself then! I'm going to take ten. Can't find the tummy tucker,' she shouted back.

I smiled.

Shruti and I had met last year at work. We were both commissioning editors at Raspberry Publishing, one of India's premier publishing houses.

We had had no choice but to hate each other. She was prettier. I was smarter. She had a better rack. I had better business knack. She had the audacity to 'accidentally' drop coffee on my desk. I had the intention to spit in her coffee the very next day.

Loathing was a way of life.

Then one fine day my landlady kicked me out because this possessive jerk that I briefly dated created a scene outside my house and Shruti took me in because her flatmate suddenly deserted her to go live with her boyfriend. We were both desperate. She needed the money. I needed a roof.

I moved in.

We began with small talk. Which grew to conversations every now and then. And then we both broke considerable ice over a drunk bare-it-all night, soon after. There was a lot of tongue and tears involved on the couch. And since that night, Shruti had kind of become a buddy. Not my best friend definitely, but a buddy for sure. Becoming a best friend takes a lot…I had a best friend once and he and I were really thick. But then…

It's funny how you suddenly remember certain people you've chosen to forget. Willingly, mostly.

I snapped out of a forgotten world to a partially filled bottle of vodka on the kitchen counter. I looked in the direction of Shruti's room once again and swiftly began to down the vodka. Neat. Alcohol came overpriced at clubs. And it was month end. Economic calculations. No hard feelings.

'That was my vodka!' Shruti had silently crept up on me.

'Umm—'

'It's okay. Let's leave. I'll have to look for an uncle now.'

'I'll help you. I promise,' I told her.

It took us a good forty-five minutes to get to Lower Parel by cab. Once outside the mall that housed the club on its fifteenth floor, Shruti looked at me and said, 'Let's hope we meet someone worth the night.'

'Yes. I could do with a pleasant surprise,' I replied.
Not knowing I had asked for more than I could digest.
Listen life, there is a difference between a pleasant surprise and a disturbing shock.
Please get your definitions right.

There's pressure involved in being a girl and living safely through it. There's chumming. There's waxing. There's staring. There's groping. Then later, there's the talk about marriage. There's the question of individual identity and misplaced equality. There's labour pain. There's the sacrifice of career. There's menopause. There's hypocrisy. But when it comes to going out and having a good time at a club, women DO have it a lot easier than men. You get to skip the serpentine queues. You don't have to pay the entry charge. You don't have to have a date to enter. The bartender often 'accidentally' pours extra alcohol in your drink. The DJ plays your requests without fail. You don't feel unwanted even if your girlfriend has met her potential guy for the night and is busy doing shots with him at the bar while you stand by her side and lazily sip your drink, for you're checking out the crowd, wondering if there is scope for that random eye-lock to happen for you.

Cute butt, sculpted muscles and some brains. That's just about it.

I scanned the crowd.

Underage boys trying hard to look like men. Men in their twenties trying hard to look underage. Boyfriends with their girlfriends, stealing guilty glances. Married men with newly married wives, confused about where their life is heading. Middle-aged men with deep pockets and bigger bellies. Gay men trying to find drunk straight prospects.

The usual.

I went for round two. The same. The same.

And then I saw…HIM. I choked on my drink. Was it really him? It couldn't be. It just fucking couldn't be. I stared hard in his direction. The same height. The same face. Or whatever I could make of it in the dim lighting. His hairstyle was different for sure. He was sporting a buzz. I remembered how much I enjoyed running my fingers through his curly locks. He was wearing a shirt. Tucked in neatly. I remembered him always complaining about how such 'formality' strangled him. He looked visibly leaner. I remembered resting my head on his broad shoulders often and how he had named his biceps just to annoy me.

It looked like him. But it didn't feel like him. Maybe he was a doppelganger. Or maybe I was just drunk and I hadn't realized it yet. Perhaps.

But then it had been five years. Five long years of no real or virtual connect. I took a few careful steps forward. And stared again. Yes, it was him! Then in the next moment, it wasn't.

My heart thumped louder than the dubstep beats the DJ and the crowd were tripping on. There was only one way to not die from a cardiac arrest tonight. I turned and waved to Shruti but she was too caught up with her catch to notice me. I said a quick silent prayer. Gulped down a large sip of my mojito. With God's prayer and his 'holy' water on my lips, I began to make my way through the crowd.

I shoved. I pushed. I elbowed. I apologized. I reached a spot from where I could see him properly, took a deep breath and narrowed my eyes in concentration, to give him a final once-over.

Seven things happened simultaneously right then.

The girl he was talking to got up from the bar stool. One.

Like a drunk bitch she almost tripped. Two.

He steadied her. Three.
I saw his face clearly. Four.
I realized it was actually HIM. Five.
He looked over her shoulder. Exactly at the spot where I was standing. Six.
Our eyes met. Fucking seven.
I quickly turned and made a dash for the smoking lounge.
Listen life, why?
It was him. It was Sumer.

We all have friends. Yet, in everyone's life, there always comes a friend, mostly when you're in school, or maybe sometimes in college, who has shaped you into what you are today.

With that friend you've shared your first smoke, your first sneak-out, got drunk for the first time and then let all your fiercely guarded emotions and thoughts flow out without the fear of judgement or an iota of embarrassment.

With that friend you've experienced the thrill of breaking rules. And shared the agony of the punishments that have followed.

With that friend you've nursed your first heartbreak. And then egged your ex's car.

With that friend you've articulated silence into a language only the two of you understand.

With that friend you've learnt the meaning of responsibility by watching out for each other even when you weren't supposed to.

With that friend you've fought volatile battles. Conducted hate campaigns against each other on Facebook. And then made up over one phone call.

With that friend you've laughed for hours over matters that the world around you doesn't give a second's importance to.

With that friend you have happy selfies, sad selfies, angry selfies, bored selfies and you can't decide if that friend, or you, knows you better.

With that friend you've learnt the wisdom of sharing pain.

With that friend you've faltered, fallen down and made mistakes only to bounce back again and learn from what went wrong. Or perhaps not.

With that friend you've found not just company but companionship.

With that friend you've lived, liked, loved, lost and learnt to live and love again.

With that friend, you've not just grown old but grown up.

You may no longer be in touch with that friend. That friend may not even be a friend anymore. But that friend continues to touch your life at levels you consciously choose to ignore.

Sumer was that friend in my life. He disciplined me like a father. He cared for me like a mother. He annoyed me like a sibling. He loved me like a boyfriend.

He was my best friend.

Some memories never die. They just fade into time. And when they come knocking at the door of reality again, you strangely wish they continued to be a distant dream.

There was a time when I couldn't think of life without him. And then there was today, when I lived a life without him.

The smoking lounge was a long, narrow, open-air alley where you could stand and admire God's concrete creation called Mumbai while you killed his mortal creation, slowly, with every drag that you inhaled.

I leant over the parapet, aimlessly staring at Mumbai's skyline, lit in the night. The loosely scattered highrises, the shanties and slums that crept up in the squeezes between them, the busy roads and the silent sea.

I took out a cigarette from my clutch and carefully placed it between my lips.

'There you go.'

I heard an achingly familiar deep and masculine voice. A flame flickered right in front of my eyes and lit my cigarette.

I took a deep drag.

'Since when did you start smoking, Tan Tan?'

I turned around. Let out a cloud of smoke. 'People change, Sumer. They grow up.'

He stepped back, as if to avoid the smoke. He lost. And coughed. Our eyes met. Again.

The sea lashed the rocks. The DJ changed the track. A random car halted with a screech. A couple in the corner took a break from their smooching session. A plane took off for its destination.

All these sounds. And the silence between us.

We continued to stare at each other. He took the few steps that distanced us. His gaze bored into me. In a swift move, his hands went around my waist, leaving me with no time to react. They held me with assurance. He pulled me closer. His head tilted a little. Lips parted. He whispered, 'Well, you surely have grown. Quite a fine pair, might I add?'

He looked at me expectantly. I could see him battling the urge to give in. But he wanted me to be the one to take the plunge first. I tried hard to keep my facial muscles in check. My throat felt dry. My heart threatened to explode. I felt the blood rush to my cheeks. I tried hard to kill the impulse. But I just couldn't.

We gave in at the same time. We burst out laughing.

'You're disgusting, Sumer!'

Just like the good old times. Pure. Uninhibited laughter.

'Come here, you.'

He didn't wait for permission. He never had to in all the years I had known him. He pulled me against his chest. I threw the cigarette on the floor as I reciprocated. It was a fuzzy, warm bear hug. Like the ones you need after a break-up or a serious bout of sickness. Or after you've lost a job. Or your dog. Or when you meet your only best friend after ages. No matter on what note you parted.

The embrace lasted till the warmth of the past faded to give way to the cold, awkward reality of the present. There was a reason why we hadn't hugged in all these years. Like all perfect friendships between a girl and a boy going wrong, we had our own story and it wasn't a pretty one. I shifted a little uncomfortably and he realized that I wanted to break the embrace. The memory of that long-ago-but-not-forgotten night had struck me again.

His arms retraced their journey and now found comfort in his pant pockets. I steadied myself. Quickly.

'How have—'

'How have—'

We both began at the same time and smiled. This time it was clearly different. Not so honest. Not so real. Like twenty-five-year-olds. The silence began to speak again.

'I'm seeing you after ages. How long has it been?' I asked mechanically, in an attempt to stop the awkwardness from spreading further.

He noticed my discomfort and smiled slightly. 'Five years, three months, twenty-two days and as we speak—' he checked his watch, 'eleven hours and twenty-three minutes and thirteen seconds. I thought you would remember.'

I was too stunned to react.

'Tanie, you know I just made up those numbers, right? Seriously, we don't stay in touch and you end up losing your sense of humour.'

I smiled, briefly.

He reached for his drink and took a sip. 'But look at you…' He checked me out again, and for the first time, it felt uncomfortable. 'All hot and pretty.'

I shot him a measured smile again. I was not quite finding the string that could tie together the words I wanted him to hear.

'And what's with this smiling business? Don't tell me you've become old and boring now, punctuating moments with smiles because you don't know what to say. C'mon now. Use words. They help.'

I simply smiled again. It was *him*. After all these years. My best friend.

He clicked his tongue in exaggerated disappointment. 'You've seriously become old. You want me to make you feel young again?' He stepped forward, dangerously close to my lips and acted as if he was going to put his arms around my waist again.

'Sumer, behave yourself!' I pushed him back, with a lot more force than I had intended to use. I instinctively held out my hand to him as he began to topple over and he caught it. And took me down with him.

'SUMER!'

Imagine blasting your favourite rock song on your new Bose speakers. Yes, that's pretty much the noise that resonated as our bodies and the glasses we were holding hit the ground. People turned around. Some stared. Some snickered. Some bitched about the drunk couple who couldn't handle their alcohol.

I lay there, partially on the ground, partially over Sumer. He must have been hurt; I had fallen right onto him. My left leg was entangled with his right one. His left arm was flung around my shoulder.

'Sumer, I'm really sor—' I began nervously, but he cut me off.

'Not bad, Tanie, that was very passionate.' He whistled to add effect.

It came from within this time. The laughter. Unlike the forced smiles that had held my face captive earlier. And the guards that I had been holding onto for all this while broke.

There's a reason why you can't ever forget the person who has hurt you the most. For deep down, beneath the layers of denial and forced smiles, you know that the same person holds the key to happiness in your life.

Sumer was that person for me. Five years ago, Sumer gave direction to how I viewed life, relationships and myself. We were best friends. And then he just left, killing our friendship, without any reason or justification. Yet today, after all these years of unanswered questions and hollow expectations, nothing seemed to matter.

Feelings that suddenly come knocking at the door of your heart are feelings that never left the comfort of it in the first place.

I continued to laugh for no reason.

'Not that I don't appreciate women on top but let's try this exercise called getting up?' He smiled.

'Oops. Sorry.' I got up quickly. And realized that we were still among a handful of people. People who were waiting for our next act, amused.

'Okay everyone, show's over,' Sumer announced.

Everyone reluctantly got back to their own conversations.

'Now that you've punished me and we're back to being normal, let's get done with the routine quickly, because I just realized I really need to take a leak.'

I faked a grimace.

'What? I meet my long-lost best friend and I can't even crack toilet jokes now?'

'Okay, shoot then, quickly.' I immediately regretted my choice of words. We laughed again.

'See, toilet jokes are always fun. Anyhow, what are you doing here? How's everyone back home? Are you still in touch with anyone from school or college? I don't see a ring, so you're not married. You look too pretty to be in an abusive relationship and if you were here with your boyfriend, he would have already fucked my happiness. So...has Tanie Brar come to a club all by herself?' He paused. 'What? You've actually come alone?'

Shruti! I had completely forgotten about her. I fished out my mobile from my clutch. Nine missed calls. *Fuck*. When I had left her with that guy she was still doing shots. Though the guy didn't look or sound shady, years of schooling in the university of heartbreak had taught me a lesson—never trust a drunk man with sap in his balls on a Saturday night.

'Um...I need to head back. I've come with a friend. I left her with a random guy...she's called nine times already and I came out here without telling her,' I said, concerned.

'How old are you girls? Sixteen?' He rolled his eyes. 'I'm sure she's fine. She must be checking on you.'

He checked his watch.

'Listen, stay put. I'll be back in two minutes. If you're still unsure, we'll go look for her together, okay?' he offered.

'Sumer—' I tried to protest.

'I'll be back in two minutes. Don't leave.'

I called Shruti and she answered my call immediately.

'I'm so sorry Shruti—'

'Tanie, you slut, who were you blowing? Anyway, just listen,' she whispered into the phone. Hurriedly.

'Are you okay, Shruti?' I panicked.

'Yes. I'm in the ladies' room. He's waiting outside and he wants to take me for a drive and it would have been totally uncool if I told him that I had to make sure you were fine...like we were sixteen-year-olds,' she scoffed.

Bitch.

'So what are you doing in the ladies' room?' I asked, confused.

'What do you think I'm doing? I came here for like the fifth time in the last twenty minutes, trying to get in touch with you so that I know you're not getting raped in a corner, while he thinks I'm suffering from a sudden bout of loosies. I couldn't find you anywhere in the club either,' she ranted.

I smiled.

'Go ahead. I'm in safe company. I met an old friend and by the looks of it, he doesn't intend to rape me. I'll meet you at home. If you're coming back tonight, that is. And please make sure he's safe. You know where to bite him if he acts weird.'

'Yes, Mamma.'

I was just about to cut the call when suddenly I felt a firm hand grab my wrist. 'What the—!' I began.

'Tanie...just run!'

Sumer cut me off as he pulled me by my arm, not giving me enough time to comprehend what he meant as he whisked me out of the smoking lounge.

'Sumer!' I shouted over the loud music, as he continued to literally drag me across the dance floor to the exit. Just as we reached it, I felt a bouncer's hand brush my shoulder.

'FUCK.' Sumer pulled me out through the exit and pushed me into the lift.

'WHO WAS THAT? WHAT DID YOU DO?' My voice boomed in the lift as I finally snapped out of my shock and caught my breath. Sumer pretended to cough, ignoring my questions. 'Stop pretending, Sumer, I know you too well.'

The lift reached the parking lot in the basement. 'Okay. Enough with the acting, will you now seriously tell me what happened?' I questioned him as he doubled up, coughing. When he didn't stop after a few seconds, I realized he wasn't pretending. I rushed to him. A copious amount of sweat had broken out on his forehead. His chest heaved in rapid breath cycles and it sounded like he was coughing from his gut. 'Are you all right?' I instinctively reached out to rub his back but he caught my hand and thrust the car key in it. The coughing got more violent with each passing second.

'Sumer!'

He pointed frantically to the key.

'What?' I asked.

'The…auto lock…pr…e…ss…it,' he managed to cough up and I immediately did as he asked. A Skoda's lights flickered a short distance away. I held his hand and started to walk him to the car as he continued to oscillate between bouts of breathlessness and coughing. As if he were having an asthma attack. Shit. That. Just that. I rushed him to the car, not realizing, in my damned inability to deal with panic, that running was the last thing he needed right now. If I hadn't bunked almost every physical education and NCC class in school and college I would have known better.

We reached his car. I made him sit on the passenger seat.

'As…th—' he tried to explain.

'I know! Stop talking and tell me, where's your inhaler?' I shouted at him, my eyes already starting to well up. Despite the heaving chest, slack mouth, racking cough, bloodshot eyes and colourless cheeks, a genuine lopsided smile spread across his face and he raised a hand, asking me to relax. He pointed to the dashboard and I lunged to open it, leaning across him. I fished through its contents, finally found the inhaler and handed it to him quickly.

Sumer grabbed the inhaler desperately. A few minutes later, he was breathing normally again. The sweat on his forehead had dried. The colour had returned to his face. He cleared his throat and reached out, wiping a solitary tear off my cheek.

'I've always wanted you between my legs.'

'Jerk.' The punch connected to something really hard, definitely not his stomach. 'Oww!' And my eyebrows arched quizzically in the very next instant. He suddenly started to unbutton his shirt. I gave him a confused look.

'What? It's not like you haven't seen it before.' He pulled out a bottle of Blue Label that was partially tucked into his pants.

'Did you—?'

'STOP, YOU THIEVES!'

The lift doors opened and my question was answered as the bouncers' voices echoed in the parking lot.

'Quick, Tanie…jump into the car and drive,' Sumer shouted.

'Huh?'

'Tanie…DRIVE!'

I yanked the stilettoes off my feet, threw them and then myself at Sumer as I climbed over the passenger's seat and into the driver's seat. He slammed the door.

'Drive, Tanie!' Sumer shouted as he saw the bouncers run towards the car.

I started the car, put it in gear, turned it around and sped away, like they do in the movies. Tonight was turning out to be just like one. The bouncers chased the car, threatening to jump on it as I cut stylishly through them and drove out of the parking lot. We got to the main road.

'Not bad, Tan Tan, your driving skills have improved. And how!'

'Why did you steal the bottle?' I demanded as I continued to drive, towards nowhere in particular.

'Oh that! So I went inside to buy a bottle of Blue Label for us. But then the bartender told me that the last bottle had just been bought by this pot-bellied burly Gujju-sari-seller-type-uncle out with his illegitimate girlfriend. I offered to buy it from him at double the price, but he just wouldn't relent. So I followed him to his table and struck up a conversation with him. And while doing so, I sneaked the bottle away.'

We stopped at a signal as I listened to him in disbelief. 'But why would you steal the bottle?' I asked, amused.

'Because it's your favourite. And tonight deserves a toast, nothing short of special.'

I was too stunned to react.

A car honked behind us. The signal had turned green.

'Drive, Tan Tan.' Sumer touched my hand briefly and I stirred and started to drive.

'You're crazy,' I said, after a few moments of silence.

'Nope. We were crazy,' he said softly.

Silence engulfed the car again.

'Take a left,' he said suddenly.

'Where to?' I questioned.

'Your place or mine?' he counter-questioned.

'Shut up!'

'So where do you live anyway?'

'Andheri, with Shruti...but...she's not coming home tonight.' He caught onto that.

'That sounded like an invitation.' I rolled my eyes.

'I live in Colaba with Mom, who you haven't particularly been interested in enquiring about,' he continued.

'You...you hardly gave me the time to...' I began to clarify.

'Chill. I'm kidding. We've not exactly shared much, yet.'

Hadn't we?

'Let's go to my house, Mom will definitely be surprised to see you.'

The thought of meeting Aarti aunty, after all these years, especially after what had happened five years ago, felt extremely strange. And the mention of her brought back memories of the past. I grew uneasy again.

'It's really late. I'll just drive to a cab and go home.'

'No way, you're not leaving so early. I'll drop you home later.'

'But Colaba and Andheri are like—'

'Miles away, but it's worth the effort. Totally,' he said softly.

I did not give him any reaction.

'You want me to get on my knees?'

'That's not enough.'

'I know. That's why I want you to stay. Will you?'

I looked away. And nodded slightly.

'So your house it is then,' he sang.

'Um...let's go to Worli Sea Face? We'll get glasses, soda and ice from this twenty-four-hour store near there... Let's do it the old-school way. Drinking by the seaside. Like we used to drink by Sukhna Lake in Chandigarh.' I smiled uncomfortably.

Sumer started to surf the radio channels, stopping at one that was playing a very old song by a singer called KK, who was popular in our schooldays back in the last decade. I remembered singing the song, drunk out of my mind, on the karaoke machine with Sumer at our unofficial class twelve farewell party.

Sumer increased the volume.

'*Yaaron, dosti, badhi hi haseen hai...yeh na ho toh, kya fir, bolo zindagi hai...*'

'You remember the farewell?' I asked fondly.

'*Koi toh ho raazdar...begaraz tera ho yaar...*' Sumer began to sing, completely out of tune, and I joined in, singing as crassly as I could. We continued to croak as I pulled up outside the store. He got the stuff in no time. We drove to Worli Sea Face.

Predictably, at 2.45 a.m., the Sea Face was populated mostly by couples. Unlike at Marine Drive, the policemen around here were relatively relaxed and though they could bust your ass if they caught you drinking, a little flash of green and a two-minute verbal banter in Marathi was all it took for them to leave you with a 'warning' and a lighter wallet.

Sumer opened the bottle and poured generous amounts of Scotch in both glasses.

'You're driving, remember?' I chided him but he chose to ignore me.

'To a night of endings and new beginnings. Let's raise a toast to all the tears, anger and the abuses we've hurled at each other in the past five years. They've got the fire in our memories burning. Let's drink to all that has kept us apart, yet so close that it doesn't feel like we've ever been apart. Let's drink to a night that won't come back again.'

'To Sumer, trying his hardest to be philosophical.'

We clinked our glasses and both of us took a large swig.

'Aaaah. Feels disgusting. This is so much like old times, Tanie.'

I smiled. It genuinely was. Sweetly disgusting.

'So tell me about everything I've missed. Done it with a girl yet? I haven't been laid in a while now.'

I wrinkled my nose in faked disgust.

'What?' he protested.

'You're mad. I've been in Mumbai for around two years. Was in Delhi and Bangalore before that. I worked with an advertising agency in Delhi for sometime but then I got bored of it. I moved to Bangalore for a bit, worked there for a magazine, started my own blog alongside, it kind of got noticed and so I got an opportunity to work for a publishing house called—'

'Raspberry Publishing Inc.'

'How do you know?' I asked, surprised, taking another sip while he played with his drink.

'Just because we don't stay in touch with each other doesn't mean I can't be in touch with what you've been up to,' he said, looking straight into my eyes.

'You chose to not stay in touch, Sumer. I was always there, you walked away. Without offering the slightest of explanations.'

The truth sprang out. It had to.

He began to say something, then pursed his lips. I silently took a sip from my glass. He stared at his feet. Guiltily.

'So...the asthma...' I began.

'Began two years ago. Pollution.'

We fell silent again. He looked around. And then finally spoke.

'So how's everyone...Uncle, Aunty, the gang?'

Family. Friends. And me. People he had left behind. Getting tired, then worn out and finally moving on, waiting for him.

'Mom and Dad are fine. So is everyone else. Stuti got married two years ago. Megha is somewhere in the US, we talk on birthdays mostly. I bumped into Shiven last year when I went back home. In fact, he was asking me if I knew where you were...but then...'

He downed his drink and poured himself another. 'Tanie...I know no apology can set right the pain I've caused you. I—'

I cut him off. 'It's okay, Sumer. I'm sure you had a reason for doing whatever you did.' I looked away from him as the buried past threatened to erupt again. 'I won't deny it hurt like a bitch. But it's okay. You left. I waited. You didn't bother connecting again. I moved on.'

The mood got sombre. The air was thick around us. The moon hid behind the clouds. And everything just felt wrong. Attempting to change the atmosphere, I began again.

'But look at you! You haven't changed a bit. Except for this hairstyle...and where's all the muscle gone?'

He stared at me. Trying hard to look through the coverings. Inside my body. He finally smiled.

'I thought you would ask deeper questions, like, what are you doing in life, Sumer? How's your mom, Sumer? But no...she wants to know where did all the meat go.'

'Idiot. So what do you do? You've got a fancy car; you're

living in a fancier locality. But wait a minute, last I knew, weren't you and Aunty going to the US to your uncle?'

'We did. But then Mom and I came back, two years ago. We're living with Nani. Mom wanted to be with her. And I...I work with my uncle now. Exports. Easy money. And then there's all the inheritance my nana left me, which I'm entitled to blow.' He smiled.

'So you never got around to making movies? It was your ultimate dream... I know it sounds crazy, but whenever I'd meet anyone from the industry socially, I would end up thinking about you.'

'If only I hadn't just left.'

A wave slapped the rocks. There, at sea. Here, between us.

'Tanie, can I ask you something? I know it's stupid. We've just met again, but can I?'

'No, we're not having sex in the car. Or in any shady corner.'

He smiled.

'First pour me a drink,' I said. He complied. I took out another cigarette. And looked at him expectantly. 'Okay to smoke?'

He lit the cigarette for me. 'So you've started smoking too, Sumer?'

'No.'

'You just lit a cigarette.'

'I got the lighter from the girl I was with at the bar. I saw you walking towards the smoking lounge.'

'Was she a friend?'

'No. As random as this night can get.'

I took a long drag. He observed me. 'What?' I queried.

'What's troubling you?' he asked as I took another drag. I choked on it. He rubbed my back. His warm hands, scaling down my spine.

'That was too strong. It hurt my throat,' I offered all too suddenly.

'I can see you're hurting,' he replied calmly.

And it unsettled me. I stubbed out my cigarette and took a sip from my drink as I felt his gaze on me. 'What?' I demanded as I suddenly felt the alcohol mixing with my blood. The buzz had started to kick in.

'The Tanie I knew didn't smoke. In fact, she detested the very sight of it,' he said and downed his drink.

'Are you judging me, Sumer? Seriously! Shouldn't I be the one to judge you? I think I should leave.' I got up.

He stopped me. 'An unlit cigarette harms more than a burnt one. A broken heart hurts less than a heart that's not experienced love.'

'Whatever that means, Sumer. I'm sorry… You have no bloody right to judge my choices in life. You should have stayed, if you cared.'

He held me firmly this time. 'Sit.'

'No.'

'Sit.'

I struggled. Our eyes locked. And we kept staring at each other.

'Sit. Hate me but sit.'

I sat down angrily and took the bottle from him.

'Let's not drink anymore.'

'What's your problem? I shouted. Blinking away the hot tears.

'Because I want us to be us for as long as we can, with undivided attention and unfiltered emotion, without the aid of anything as low as alcohol…'

Silence. Heavy panting. Both ends. And that's when it happened. We both inched forward. Our lips met. Ever so softly. Like we wanted to feel every sensation, each tangled breath. Together. Our tongues collided as we exchanged all the unsaid, unheard tales of the past five years that we hadn't got the opportunity to share. Cinderella. Sleeping Beauty. Rapunzel. And now Tanie. The fairy-tale kiss lasted for not more than a skip or two of a second's hand. I let my eyes stay shut, meditating on a feeling I had long forgotten.

'It's time to leave,' Sumer said suddenly in a hoarse voice and I opened my eyes. He walked back briskly to the car. I followed him slowly, confused. He got into the driver's seat and I sat beside him, even more confused. He drove in silence. I stole a few glances at him, but he kept his attention on the road, like I didn't exist in the car. Or in his world. All over again.

As we reached Andheri, he mechanically asked for directions and I mumbled them. 'Right here. The third building on the left. That's where I live.' He stopped the car with a jerk. I got out, half expecting him to spring out and say, 'Tanie, how did you like this intense acting piece? I was just making sure you took me to your house.' But as I shot him a final expectant look, he glanced at me briefly, mumbled a soft 'goodbye' and sped off.

The confusion made way for anger.

They say if you ever leave someone, at least leave them with an explanation. Abandonment brings misery. Knowing you're not even worth an explanation is the real pain.

He had done it again! The second time in five years. I was pissed at him. Like killing Taliban pissed. Like castrating rapists pissed. Like slapping bitches with fake accents pissed. Like asking flop directors to stop making movies pissed. PISSED.

Buzzed with all the alcohol and boiling with all the anger in me, I made my way to my flat. I lit a cigarette and puffed on it quickly as I went directly to the kitchen and looked through all the cabinets, searching for more alcohol. I found a bottle of Old Monk and took a few sips. After the last sip, I smoked another cigarette as I walked to my room, sloshed.

I remember hitting my foot against the sofa or banging into the cupboard in my room. I remember getting hurt somewhere by something for sure. I remember the pain. I remember the tears. I remember slumping on my bed. I remember lying there for a while. My head refusing to stop spinning. I remember shouting out his name.

'SUMER!'

I remember remembering all the times we spent together, the memories we carved, the decisions we took, the fuck-ups we created. I remembered how we became friends, how he ended it and how I had had no choice but to accept the decision. I remember remembering our kiss today. I remember remembering the first time we had kissed at sixteen. I remember remembering our story.

Part 2

Lived. Liked. Loved.
And then I lost him.

The year was 2010. Justin Bieber had hit puberty, or so he claimed. People still bought Nokia mobile phones. Onions hadn't crossed the price of beer. People were done booing Hi5 and had just scrapped Orkut. MySpace didn't catch the Indian fancy. A geek in Harvard had just struck gold with a book everyone wanted their faces on. People still nudged over MSN, buzzed on Yahoo and pinged on Google messenger. BBM had come along, but hadn't yet erupted. WhatsApp hadn't yet entered India and 'last seen at' were still three simple words strung together into a harmless sentence that did not threaten to ruin your relationship.

I was sixteen. And living every one of the stereotypes associated with that age. Secret calls with my girlfriends, Stuti and Megha. Disagreeing with my mother on practically everything. Bursting pimples and stuffing my bra with equal fervour. Dreading the pending declaration of my tenth-grade Board examination results. Indulging, then regretting and yet again indulging in life-changing gossip.

The problems of life at sixteen were…different. Monsters still lived under the bed, and not on them. Bad bosses, shitty jobs, paying the electricity bill on time, alcohol poisoning, failed friendships, lost love or fighting pangs of loneliness weren't issues that plagued life.

In 2010, life posed simple questions. Whom to love? Whom to be friends with? And I had ended up confusing the answer. Dangerously.

After breaking up with my boyfriend, Rehaan, I had kissed my best friend, Sumer.

Sumer…

Our friendship was as unusual as our first few interactions had been. In the summer of 2009, I was walking back from English tuition when two creepy-looking boys from my tuition class zipped past me on their Honda Activa, catching me totally unawares. I pulled off a classical 'me'—landing on the road on all fours. A tall muscular guy with curly hair came to my rescue, scooping me up off the road. I mumbled a quick thank-you and left.

That guy turned out to be my new neighbour and we were acquainted in the 'barest' sense that very night, as my family was invited for dinner to his place. I had been asked to fetch him from his room. And what happened next scarred me for the rest of my life.

After knocking repeatedly on his door I politely opened it, only to find him dancing in his boxers. Just his boxers.

Then my neighbour not only joined the school neighbouring mine—the only boys' convent in Chandigarh—but also landed up at almost all the same tuitions that I went to.

We began with carpooling for school. Then for tuitions. Then my friends met him. I met his friends. My friends met his friends. Permutations and combinations. And our gang was formed.

As the calendar kept tripping on months, Sumer and I became best friends. In the truest form. Just that, though. I was dating Rehaan, my first boyfriend, at that time and Sumer was in a long-distance relationship with this girl called Liaka. And then, one fateful cold December morning, I found out that Rehaan was cheating on me. Sumer came to my rescue as I cried my eyes out after my first heartbreak. He held me in his arms while I shivered and wiped my nose on his shirt.

And then we kissed.

And Sumer suddenly came up with the idea that he loved

me. I completely cut off from him. At the time I thought I loved Rehaan and kissing Sumer had made me feel like a…slut.

Heartbreak was still a novelty back then.

January. February. March. We didn't share as much as a 'hello' for three long months after that kiss. I avoided him at all costs. And avoiding him meant pretty much boycotting my social life. I stopped hanging out with the gang. Stopped going for birthday parties. Avoided his calls, his texts. Deleted him from Facebook. Went to the tuitions only when I needed to and then sat in the first row, always, with the nerds. Our friends did occasionally wonder what had happened between the two of us, but with the Boards round the corner, they were too busy studying to dig too deep.

Education had ruined us.

As soon as the Boards ended, I enrolled myself for a MUN conference in Singapore. (For the uninitiated, MUN or Model United Nations is a simulation of how the United Nations works, where students debate as representatives of different countries on issues that trouble the world. In reality, it was a student fest where teenagers dressed up in their formal best and hooked up left, right and centre.) The night before I was to go to Singapore for this 'academic' competition, Sumer suddenly popped in and gave me a letter. In his illegible handwriting. He asked me a simple question in it—*can a girl and boy just be friends?*

And as strange as it may sound, I found the answer to the question on the flight back from Singapore. From a stranger who shared a story with me. About his life.

Aaryan.

He also had a best friend, Boza, and Ishita, a girl whom he thought he loved. He had gone to Singapore for her but on the day his flight landed there, he had found out that Boza had been in a serious accident back in India. She had been badly injured and was still in the ICU as we landed in India, a week after the accident. He left me with a poem Boza had written, revealing all that she felt for him. And I found my answer to Sumer's question in that poem.

I sent Aaryan a friend request on Facebook as soon as I reached home. He declined it. I sent him another request—I wanted to know what had happened to Boza. He blocked me this time. I then searched for Boza's profile, but couldn't find it.

That's the thing about trying to form a bond with a stranger. It snaps as soon as you try to make it personal.

Maybe Aaryan had wanted it to stay this way. Maybe he had lost Boza. Maybe this was his way of telling me I shouldn't lose Sumer. And so I finally decided to go to Sumer's house and answer his question.

Can a girl and a boy just be friends?

I regretted ringing the doorbell of his house the moment I pressed it. Chickening out, I turned to leave but just then the door opened.

'Tanie? What a surprise! Where were you going?' Even his mom was stunned to see me.

Premature ejaculations and bad beginnings. They never end happily ever after.

'Hi Aarti aunty, is…is Sumer there?' I wished she would say 'no'. But then granted wishes are like good hair days. Rare. And unheard of.

'Come in, beta. Sumer's inside…I haven't seen you forever!'

'Aunty, I—'

I found myself being pulled inside with an enthusiasm that only she could have managed at this lazy hour. So here's the deal with Aarti aunty. Unlike her stern, strict navy captain of a husband, she was a ship of energy that never quietly anchored at shore.

I trailed into the living room behind her and was politely pushed onto the sofa. The box of imported chocolates I had picked up from the pantry, where all the leftover Diwali gifts from last year were kept, fell down in the process. I was obviously going to lie and tell Sumer that I had bought them in Singapore, especially for him.

'Oh. I'm sorry—' Aarti aunty sprang up from her seat and picked up the box.

'It's okay, Aunty.' I smiled nervously. My eyes wandered to the staircase where Sumer and I had kissed. I kept staring at it as Aunty continued to shoot question after question at supersonic speed.

'So, beta, how was your trip? When did you come back? Why haven't you been visiting in the last few months? Did you and Sumer fight? I asked him but he denied it completely... How's Mom? I haven't seen her in sometime as well... How did your Board exams go? Are you scared about the result?'

She finally paused to breathe (surprise!) and realized that I hadn't come here to gossip with her. She leaned forward and touched my hand. 'You want me to call Sumer?'

'Sorry... What?'

'Tanie, you want me to call Sumer?' She looked at me gravely.

'I'll just go to his room.' It took a mammoth effort to fake a smile, shooting down any suspicion that may have arisen in her mind thanks to my erratic behaviour. The last thing I wanted was for his mother to be a referee while we discussed why we had indulged in an intense match of tonsil tennis.

Aunty studied my expressions secretly. Parents do that all the time. I knew the look.

'Sure, beta, go ahead. I'll ask Shanti to make some cold coffee for you kids.'

I smiled at her briefly, got up and went to his room.

Nervous, brimming with anticipation, I gently knocked on the door of his room. He didn't respond. The second round of knocking was louder, its bold sound resonating in the hallway. Still no response. Carefully I turned the doorknob. It was unlocked. I peeked in and saw him sitting on the edge of his bed with his back to the door and his face to the wall.

Our picture hung there. The one we had taken on his birthday last year. That was the first time I had got permission to go for a late-night birthday party and, like the perfect teenage daughter, I made sure my parents regretted giving it to me.

Sumer's father was going to foot the bill, so there was no way we could order anything with even a trace of alcohol in it. But Sumer had come prepared, hiding miniature bottles from his father's bar in his pockets. We all ordered a lot of Coke that night. And mixed it with all the vodka and whisky. Both of which I had for the first time.

It began with uncontrollable giggling. Then came the hiccups. And then, just as everyone was scaring Sumer about plastering his face with the birthday cake, I decided to garnish it. As Sumer was about to cut the cake, my stomach revolted.

Sumer happily cut the cake afterwards, openly challenging everyone to unleash the artist within them and decorate his face just as they pleased. The noses wrinkled. The eyes reflected disgust. I dug my hand in the chocolate-vodka-Tanie saliva cake and plastered it on Sumer's face. Sumer picked up a bigger slice and gave me a facial. Chunks of cake flew all around. And the just-hatched drunk sixteen-year-olds started a cake fight amongst the entire gang. Expensive shirts. Classy make-up.

Gelled hair. Dry-cleaned dresses. Just-discovered high heels. Fake logo belts. All soiled. And then, as we were clicking pictures in all our disgusting glory, for Facebook, of course, the management at the lounge sneakily called in Sumer's parents.

Sumer's dad smelled the alcohol as soon as he marched in. All the parents were called to his house that night. I was grounded. Sumer was slapped. The other parents also oscillated between the two options. And Sumer being Sumer had gone ahead and got our picture from that night framed and put it up on his wall, just to piss his father off. Their relationship was like that. One in which china broke, forks flew and doors slammed, often whenever his father came back from a sail. His father was the stereotypical navy captain. Back straight. Tie, with a single knot, touching the tip of the belt, fork and spoon for tandoori chicken. Wine after dinner. Handkerchief folded and placed in the right pocket. While Sumer was, well, an anomaly who'd clearly skipped his father's gene pool.

Even as I saw him, his curly locks, falling over his ears, could be combed and pulled back into a neat ponytail. The loose T-shirt, the lanky yet muscular arms, the tattoo that he had hidden from his parents, the casual drop of the shoulders—he was made to define laid-back.

I cleared my throat to speak. 'Sumer.'

He didn't stir. Not even by an inch.

'Sumer...' No reaction. Like he didn't know I was in the room. Yes. That's exactly what was happening here. Pretence. The oldest trick in the book. I began again patiently. 'Sumer, I know you can hear me,' I shook the box of chocolates I had brought for him. That should definitely get a reaction. 'Sumer...look, I got you food.' The trick always worked on my Labrador when she threw a tantrum.

My Labrador likes food. Sumer likes food. Sumer is a Labrador. Simple. Deductive logic.

He did not even react to the call for food! HIM, of all the

animals that I knew. I took a deep breath. 'Sumer. Can you stop pretending, please?' He still sat there, unperturbed.

Anger, much like untimely erections, often finds a way to screw the mind.

With every intention of kicking his balls so hard that they would swell to become bigger than the ice packs he would later use on them, I walked up to him. I put a firm hand on his shoulder and just as I turned him around...

Things that should never, ever, ever, ever, ever have happened—happened. Shanti, the maid, walked in with the glasses of cold coffee. Sumer turned. Our eyes met.

'Sumer!' I yelled. In anger.

'Tanie!' he exclaimed. In surprise.

Shanti saw us look at each other. In shock. The coffee glasses fell from her hand. I froze.

'Tanie, I'm sorry!' he shrieked.

'Tanie didi, sorry!' So did Shanti.

Sumer dashed to the washroom. The maid dashed out of the room. The box of chocolates fell from my hand. The box of tissues Sumer had kept nearby fell, right next to where his mobile, with the earphones attached to it, had fallen a few moments ago, when Sumer had jumped off his bed. My eyes went to his mobile's screen as I stood there transfixed, too confused to decide what to do next.

'Naughty America. Nobody does it better.' A muscular guy continued eating a petite girl's face. The screen glowed. The girl moaned louder. My heart sank deeper. And hit the Titanic debris.

I had come to discuss a kiss that shouldn't have happened with my best friend. Then I wanted to kick him in the balls. And in the end, I had ended up seeing another kiss and another pair of balls.

Dear life, why?

A long hot shower. A deep-tissue body massage. Having good prolonged sex. Writing poetry. Listening to rock music. Doing t'ai chi. Painting. Cutting yourself. Draining warm Scotch neat. Going for a long walk on the beach. Rolling a joint. Meditation. Different people do different things to space out from their thoughts and find perspective. I chose running. Track shorts. Hair tied up. Headphones plugged in, reverberating with the sound of my workout playlist. I ran, lap after lap, wanting my feet to ache.

Buzzz. Buzzzz. Buzzzzzzzzz. My cell phone vibrated, yet again, and I let it be. The call died, taking the toll of missed calls to twenty-eight. *Buzz. Buzz.* I jerked to a halt and decided to finally answer the call.

'Listen...I...don't...want to talk right...now,' I panted heavily into the phone.

'Why? Because I bought the dress at Zara that you were eyeing?' Megha's squeaky voice hit my ears. The anger subsided. It wasn't him.

'Exactly why, Megha,' I offered as I checked the time on my watch. It was half past seven and it had gotten dark enough for Mom to start hyperventilating about the apocalypse that night brought for 'young' girls out on the streets. This, after Chandigarh was judged as one of the safest cities in the country by some nationwide poll last year. Melodrama runs in the DNA of Punjabi moms. I walked out of the park, which was near my house.

'Why do you sound so flustered?' Megha asked.

'I had come for a run,' I replied, flicking a bead of sweat off my forehead.

'Oh. Why?'

Coz I just caught my best friend shagging away to glory. Just when I had gone to discuss the tissues, I mean issues, that had cum, I mean come, between us. And I wanted to get the disturbing visual out of my mind!

'Just. Felt. Like. It,' I answered instead, kicking a pebble as I continued to walk towards home. The street was devoid of activity. There were a few cars parked in front of houses. At a distance, a maid stood with a guy whom I suspected to be her lover. A little ahead, an old man was trying to relive his youth by trying his best at brisk walking.

'Umm...Tanie. I wanted to ask you something,' Megha continued in a grave tone. 'I know you hate talking about this...but did you and Sumer fight because of Rehaan?'

I stopped, irritated. Now that the Boards were over, everyone suddenly wanted to get back to the world of frivolous gossip.

'Megha, can I tell you something, but you have to promise me you won't tell this to anyone? It's a secret.' I imagined her doing an excited somersault already. Gossip Girl. Enough said.

'Sumer, Rehaan and I, we were having a threesome. Suddenly Sumer pushed me away and started to suck Rehaan instead. And Rehaan enjoyed it, even more surprisingly. I realized both of them are meant for each other, so I let the two of them be,' I said in the most serious tone I could come up with. She was at a loss for words. I smiled sadistically.

'Umm, you sure there's nothing wrong with you?' Megha spoke finally.

'Megha, I'm fine. Can we not talk about what I don't want to talk about?'

'Sure...I was just checking if Sumer is...'

'If Sume—'

A Ford Endeavour came out of nowhere and screeched to a halt right in front of me.

'What was that noise?' Megha questioned, confused.

Before I could reply or make sense of what was happening, the car's back door opened and a guy wearing a monkey cap pulled me in. I had no time to react as the car accelerated away. Inside, another guy, who was sitting in the front seat, turned around and snatched my phone away. A balloon of fear burst inside me and I tried to shout, but nothing came out of my mouth. I took a deep breath and tried to shout from my belly this time, but nothing came out again.

'Don't shout or I will stab you!' a coarse voice instructed me as I felt something being poked in my stomach. For a moment I thought I had heard the voice before, but common sense prevailed and I rubbished the thought as a déjà vu moment. I looked around frantically. This was a goddamn residential area. There were houses on both sides of the street. '*You're not home, Tanie! And it's already dark.*' Mom's voice echoed in my head and I felt my eyes well up. I blinked hard as reality hit me. This wasn't a re-creation of a kidnapping on prime-time television with bad actors and over-dramatized situations. I was actually being kidnapped!

I tried to wrestle my way out of the car but the guy on my side overpowered me, holding my hands.

'HELP!' The shout came from within. And this time it was loud. But my voice bounced off the rolled-up tinted windows and slapped me back with the sinking reality of the situation.

'HELPPPPPPP!' I shouted helplessly again. And out of instinct, I sunk my teeth into the guy's shoulder as I struggled to get my hands free from his tight clasp.

'Ouch, dude, she bit me!' This time the voice sounded even more familiar.

'Tanie…you bad, bad girl,' the guy sitting in the front seat suddenly began to sing. Laughter filled the car as I sat there, not processing even an iota of what was happening around me.

The two men took off their monkey caps. Shiven! Viraaj! Just then the car halted and the driver turned around and took off his monkey cap as well.

'WHAT THE HELL, SUMER!' In a flash, I found myself reflexively grabbing the knife Shiven was holding in his hand and lunging for Sumer.

'Woahh...Tanie!' I heard Shiven shout. His eyes grew big with fear. Viraaj squealed.

'Ahhhhhh!' Sumer bawled.

'I'm so sorry, Sumer...' I began, only to be silenced by laughter. Yet again.

'It's a butter knife, Tan Tan,' Sumer winked and pulled the knife out of my hand.

'THIS IS BLOODY NOT FUNNY!' I screamed. The laughter stopped. The car screeched to a halt. Viraaj and Shiven carefully got out of it.

'Just. Drop. Me. Home. Sumer.' I rolled down a window, looked around and realized we weren't very far from home. He had just circled the neighbourhood. 'WHERE IS MY PHONE?' Shiven slid it through the window to me. 'WAIT TILL MEGHA HEARS ABOUT THIS!' I barked at him. Megha and Shiven had been doing each other for the longest time, yet weren't 'together' together.

'But it was all Sumer's idea...I just followed suit,' Shiven yelped.

I switched my phone on, ignoring him, and checked if Mom had called.

'I sent your parents and my mom for a movie. They won't be back before ten,' Sumer offered, as though reading my mind.

'YOU. Shhhh.' I thrust a finger on his lips and dialled another number.

'Dude, is she calling the cops?' I heard Viraaj whisper to Shiven. Shiven shot him a look of disgust.

'The number you're trying to reach is busy on another call—'

Sumer's mobile rang just then. 'Hi Megha,' he began carefully.

I snatched the phone from his hand. 'Megha...I was just calling you—'

'Tanie, I got so scared, your call got cut and your number wasn't reachable and...and I didn't know what to do... I thought of calling your mom but then I thought she would panic, so...I called up Sumer,' she ended in a tiny voice, sounding more panicked than even I had been when I was being held hostage at the end of a goddamn butter knife.

'It's fine, Megha. Everything is fine. I'll call you later and explain everything,' I said to calm her down.

'Okay,' she said and then as an afterthought added, 'But how are you with Sumer?'

'It's a long story...I'll call you in some time.' I looked at Shiven and added, 'Megha, I don't know how to break this to you, but I think I saw Shiven's car today. I think he was with someone. Check his neck...maybe.' I cut the call and smiled sinisterly at Shiven, who glared at Sumer, who in turn gasped at what I had just done.

'Will you drop me home now, Sumer?' I said in a firm non-emotional voice.

'But what about us? How do we get home?' I heard Viraaj complain to Shiven, who was already on a call with...*drum rolls, spotlight*...Megha. Viraaj got the finger in response from me, as Sumer started the car and looked apologetically at his friends.

'Beers on me, for the entire month,' he promised them as the car started to move. 'Tanie, I—'

'Don't, Sumer,' I cut him off.

He took a turn around the curb. I could see our houses up ahead.

'Tanie—'

'Sumer, no, you've pissed me off enough already!' A dog came in front of the car, out of nowhere, and he suddenly braked. I was jerked forward and my forehead hit the windscreen. 'Oww,' I growled.

'Oh my God! Sorry, Tanie.'

'Can you decide what all you're apologizing for?' I snapped, nursing my forehead. He stared at me. His eyes all emotional. Lips pursed in a silent plea. 'What?' I battled hard to hold on to my anger, but his gaze was doing a good job of melting it away.

'I'm sorry for everything that I have done to hurt you,' he said, with earnest eyes. 'You weren't taking my calls, so I called up your place and Aunty told me you had gone for a jog, so I made this plan…I think I should stop watching all the South Indian movies they dub in Hindi and show on Sony Max all the time.'

He knew it was a good joke. I tried to not flex my jaw muscles in response. Sumer started the car again and drove to my house in silence. He stopped outside my house. I looked at my watch. 8.35 p.m. They weren't going to return before ten. This idiot had planned it out well.

'Do you want some coffee?' I asked him.

'Um…'

'What?'

'Can we do beer instead? We'll buy some from this liquor shop nearby. Shiven and I discovered it last month. The guy doesn't ask for ID, it's totally underground. We'll get back and gargle before our parents return,' he offered in a tiny voice.

'You…' I paused and took a painfully long breath before continuing, 'Why do we need beer?'

'Because coffee is unhealthy,' he offered impulsively.

'And they make beer at the gym,' I snapped back.

'Because you won't judge me once you're drunk, Tanie,' he found the words escaping his mouth.

Despite the situation, a smile crept across my face. 'Beer it is, then.'

He smiled. We drove to the shop. He bought two Millers.

'You didn't congratulate me on my new car,' he commented as he yanked off the bottle caps with his teeth.

'Congratulations. Thanks for trying to kidnap me in it,' I replied.

He went red in the face again. 'You wouldn't take my calls. You know how difficult it was to execute the entire plan? Send our folks to the movies, get the car out without Mom's permission… You know she would have flipped and called Dad! Then I had to convince Shiven and Viraaj…arrange for monkey caps…they are Viraaj's dead grandfather's…'

I tried hard not to laugh out loud. I didn't want him to win so soon. We continued to sip from our beer bottles. And then finally, after I was done drinking half the bottle, I decided to begin the conversation that should have happened way earlier. Sans the drama of the entire day.

'Sumer—' I cleared my throat. 'Don't interrupt me when I say this, okay?'

He looked up at me cutely, the bottle stuck to his mouth.

'Sumer, I'm sorry that we kissed, okay? I really like you but I don't love you. Like, I mean I love you but not in the way I'm supposed to love you and I know you just love me in the same way as I love you because you think you love me in the way you love me but that's not how we love each other. So stop loving me the way you think you love me and start liking me the way I think you love me…' Phew! There…finally…I had got it out of my system. I took a large sip from the bottle.

'Tanie,' he took a dramatic gulp from his bottle and began in all seriousness, 'I…I lost you the second time you said, "I love you".' He burped without covering his mouth.

'Sumer, seriously?' I grimaced but he suddenly brought a hand to my lips. Staring intently at me, he spoke. 'Tanie, I don't know what you were thinking about when we kissed each other but I know what I felt just then. Or how I have been feeling for the past four months.' He continued to stare into my eyes, his hand still stuck to my lips.

Being with Sumer made me smile but I still cried to Rehaan's memories when I was alone.

That kiss had felt special. Very special. But it was just a moment. And by definition, it had no business overstaying its purpose.

Taking his hand into mine, I began, 'Look, Sumer. You're my best friend. You're the guy whom I can meet on a bad hair day and still not feel conscious about it. You're the guy I want to call at 4 a.m. when I'm not sleepy and discuss how my tits are growing uneven and get some male perspective on it, not the guy who wakes me up at 4 a.m. by fondling them. You're the guy I want to have candid pictures with on Facebook, not the guy for whom I have to Photoshop them. You're the guy who will protect me from other guys, not the guy who can snap my heart in a moment. You're the guy I can pass out drunk with, in the same room, and still get up next morning confident that you wouldn't touch me—'

'I'm not sure about the passing-out-drunk-bit, alcohol can make you do things. Dirty things,' he interjected.

I smiled briefly. Knowing he obviously meant otherwise. 'You're the guy I want to spend my Sunday afternoons with, lazing around in my oversized T-shirt, on my couch, watching *The Return of Indra*, or *Shivaji No. 1*, or even better, *Playboy— Ek Mawali ki Love Story*. Not the guy I want to watch *Twilight* with, fingers entwined and heartbeat irregular. You're the guy I want to discuss my relationship problems with, not the guy I want to create a relationship problem with. With you I can be real, Sumer…that's the best part about our friendship.'

'Tanie, we could be everything that you want us to be… What makes you think if we date, we won't be able to keep it real?' he argued.

'You spilled some beer on your shirt,' I commented.

'That's okay. It's used to soaking up my tears anyway.'

He looked at me. I looked at him. And we both burst out laughing.

'Sheesh, Sumer, that was SO creepy.'

'I know, right… Damn, I sounded so gay.'

'Sumer, this is exactly what I'm saying, just look at this… Aren't we sorted this way?' I grinned.

'Hmmm… Do you still think about him, Tanie?'

And the grin died. I could have lied to him. It would have hurt him less. But…

'I do. He might have cheated on me, Sumer, but my feelings were genuine. They still are.'

Sumer looked away. After what seemed like a decade, he spoke, very softly. 'In that case, I'm sorry, Tanie…I don't think this will work out between us.'

My heart sank. 'What do you mean?' I whispered.

'You can't be sitting in a car so close to me and not expect me to want to kiss you…' He winked.

I smiled. From the deepest recess of my heart.

He finished his beer, reversed the car and drove me back to my house. Just as I was about to get out of the car, he pulled me back inside and curled his arms around my waist.

'What are you doing, Sumer? Someone will see us!'

'But now that I've been single for four long months… Can't I sometimes just touch you inappropriately?'

'How about a "no"?' I freed myself and got out.

'We can be just friends, only on one condition,' he shouted from the car.

I looked around, not wanting anyone to hear us. 'What?' I asked hurriedly.

'You have to tell me who was a better…' he whispered the last word, 'kisser?'

'Goodbye, Sumer.'

He honked again. 'Tanie…so who was bigger, him or me…now that you've seen both?'

'I only taste and tell,' I winked back.
He smiled. She smiled. Problem solved.

Like sunrise and sunset. Like my messy cupboard. Like Sumer PMSing over his father's impending arrival. Like stalking Rehaan to keep tabs on his new girlfriend. Like trying to get a lead on Aaryan, the guy I met on the flight from Singapore, so I could ask him about Boza's condition. Like Arnab Goswami's daily rants. Like Rakhi Sawant's latest surgery. Life fell quietly and comfortably into routine after that night.

The kiss was history. Our friendship, the present. Sure, Sumer did go through the occasional moonlight moment but I was always alert to bring in enough sunshine every time he looked funnily at me, whenever we had a moment. In his room. In his car. In my backyard. At the coffee shop. Or the liquor store we used to get alcohol from.

April dissolved into May. And May trickled over to June.

'I wish the Somali pirates had captured his ship and held him hostage just till tomorrow,' Sumer texted me the morning before the Board results were to be declared, when he saw his father standing in his room at 5.30 a.m. He had 'surprised' Sumer with an unannounced visit.

That evening the entire gang met at Sumer's house. He sneaked into his father's room and stole a bottle of Old Monk from his cupboard. Shanti got the Coke, glasses and ice. And later the lemons. All of us knew we weren't going to get any sleep till we poisoned our blood. The trick worked.

The next morning, as the sun was just beginning to kick the night out of the sky, I was woken up by Sumer's call. As it turned out, the CBSE had got an early morning boner. I had scored an 87 per cent, Sumer told me as soon as I groggily answered the phone, hungover. I had scored a fucking 92 in maths. I shrieked so loudly that Mom and Dad rushed to my room. Sumer had scored an 80 per cent. My parents were overjoyed with our scores. His father was dismissive about his score. But that wasn't the real problem.

'Filmmaking is uncertain, have a back-up plan. Get an engineering degree, you have the potential to crack a good engineering college,' Sumer croaked an adolescent impersonation of his father's much deeper voice.

We were in his backyard. He was shooting hoops while I looked on.

'Vikram has no heart; my mother married him for his inheritance. And she's sold her otherwise chirpy voice to his soul. He wants me to take up non-medical! Just out of nowhere, he wants me to become an engineer! He knows I can't study for hours and mug up endless books! That's just not my scene. And there's a reason why I've only asked for expensive video cameras on my birthday, year after year. Filmmaking is my scene. New York Film Academy, that's where I have to go eventually.' He missed the shot.

'But they knew of what you've wanted to do all along!'

'Turns out, only your parents understand what you want to do. Dad said that just because he never stopped me from wasting my time with the camera, doesn't mean he thinks it could be a career for me. It's just a hobby. And you know what's the worst part, even Mom isn't taking my side! She says Vikram knows best for me, even if I don't understand it right now. I even threatened to run away but he didn't budge, knowing I wouldn't. He won't change his decision. I know him.' He missed another shot.

'That means we won't even go to the same school now?'

'Fuck you, Tanie! That's all you care about. If Vikram has his way, I'll have to suffer for the next six years. He's asked me to do whatever I want *after* the engineering degree.'

He threw the ball hard and it bounced back off the ring, hitting him in his face. He fell down. Despite the tension, I burst out laughing.

'My father doesn't understand me. My future is doomed. And my best friend is laughing at that. Perfect,' he grumbled.

I got up and nursed him. 'Try talking to Uncle again. You can't just get into non-medical. He's just concerned and let's be honest, considering you, you really can't blame him, you've always been a pain in the ass for him, Sumer. Talk to him politely, with a smile, not a scowl, hug him like I hug my dad without any reason, not coz you want some money.'

Sumer's eyes were liquid.

'He's on an ego trip. I know him.'

He hugged me, his muffled breaths tingling the hair on the nape of my neck. I reciprocated and rubbed his back warmly. I knew he wanted to cry out loud but was just being macho about it.

'You're crushing my tits.'

'I know.'

I pushed him away playfully and he smiled.

'You want me to talk to Aunty?'

He contemplated.

'I don't think that'll help. It's like Dad's getting back at me for everything wrong that I've done to him.'

A tear escaped his eye. I wiped it for him. He touched my hand.

And then, I don't know why, our faces inched forward. And then...

'Sumer!'

We heard a stern voice. I got up immediately. Sumer followed suit. His father's muscular imposing six-foot frame approached us. I kept staring down, too scared to meet his gaze.

'Tanie.'

I looked up, petrified. Uncle's face broke into a smile. Like he hadn't seen us almost kiss. Or maybe he actually hadn't. Yes, that.

'You're an intelligent girl. Why don't you fill some sense in your friend here?' He shot a stern glance at Sumer and Sumer stared back at him with unnerving intensity.

'I need to go,' I said quickly, before they got out their ninja swords and killed each other.

'I'll walk you out.' Sumer caught my hand and we walked out to his gate. 'Listen...sorry for that, inside.'

'It's okay...it was just...I mean...we're friends...you know...happens.'

'Oh. I wasn't talking about the...I mean...sorry for Dad...'

'Yes, okay.'

'Yeah.'

'Tell me what Uncle says.'

'I will.'

'Don't worry. He'll understand.'

'If he doesn't, will your parents adopt me?'

'I doubt that. But you could totally sell your body for sustenance.'

'That's a great idea. Why don't I try out my skills on you?'

'Bye. Call me after you tell him. If you want, I can come for support.'

'I will.'

Sumer didn't call me that day. In fact, his struggle continued till the end of June. After a lot of broken china, quarrelling, door slamming, threats of leaving the house and the sinking realization that reality wasn't much like a Bollywood movie, where you could just leave your house and work your ass off breaking stones on a mountain, his father passed the verdict. Sumer was going to study science. And become one of the jerk-offs who smoked weed and played Counter-Strike with a beer belly in the name of studying engineering.

His father had even taken his video camera away, just before he left for a sail. The night Uncle left, Sumer broke into his bar, flicked some fancily named expensive wine and we sneaked out of our houses to go drink in the nearby park. We drank from the bottle as we sat on the swings. The wine tasted horrible. But that wasn't the reason why the mood was sombre. In fact, Sumer hadn't looked so depressed even when he broke up with his girlfriend, Liaka. Or when his Internet had been down for two straight porn-free weeks last year.

The silence was annoying me. And the mosquitoes weren't helping either.

'Umm…do you want me to flash my tits, if it makes you feel any better?' He didn't smile even at that. 'You know, I'm not wearing a bra.' His head didn't turn. He was genuinely disturbed. I let him be and sat there silently by his side. Fighting the mosquitoes as he battled his demons. After a few minutes, he suddenly spoke.

'Do you think I'm adopted?'

'What?'

'Do you think I'm adopted, Tanie?'

'Err…if they were to adopt a kid, wouldn't they want a good-looking baby instead?' He finally smiled. Briefly, though.

'I don't understand my own father, Tanie. I agree I've been quite a dick, all my life, but this isn't a fight about if I will wear my pajamas or not to dinner at his friend's place—'

'You wore pajamas to dinner at his friend's place!'

'I didn't feel like changing.'

'I don't really blame him, you know—'

He rolled his eyes.

'This is serious. I know what this is about. His ego. He knows this is the only way he can get back at me.'

'Look,' I began very cautiously. 'Think from his perspective. He does have a point, you know…he's a grown-up man, and you're just a spoilt brat.'

Sumer looked at me in disbelief. Like I had just grown a pair of balls. And asked him to touch them.

'HE DOES NOT. I'm not doing non-medical. I might be a little...' he paused to find the correct word.

'Indulgent?' I offered.

He made a face. 'Fine, indulgent in life...but...I'm not doing something I don't want to do. And what about this?' He groped his crotch.

'Yuck, Sumer!'

'Oh, come on! Just think about it, there won't be any girls around, neither right now nor later in college, if I end up doing engineering. I'll die of excessive sperm production, if not a nervous breakdown.'

'You do have a solid hand in making your future, you know. Pun intended.'

He laughed before turning pensive again. A mosquito bit me on my neck. And I let it go. The sacrifices we make for friendship.

'Let's leave.'

We walked back to our houses.

Just before we reached my house, Sumer suddenly stopped and spoke.

'You know what? I'm going to do science for two years now and I'll study hard enough to build his hopes, and just when he thinks he's got it all under control, I will screw up my twelfth Boards and entrances and then it's going to be film school for me.'

I didn't like the sound of how coldly he wanted to exact revenge on his father. 'Sumer, you sure about this? I mean you could still talk to him, you know.'

'Listen, stop patronizing me. You're supposed to be my best friend, not his.'

'I'm not patronizing you, all I'm saying is—'

'That I'm going to study science now and show him who's

the daddy. You won't judge me, right?' He looked at me expectantly, waiting for my answer. A car came out of nowhere and honked at us. Luckily, it wasn't someone from the locality.

'Listen, let's go back inside before someone sees us.'

'Would you judge me or not, Tanie?'

I looked at the wine bottle in his hand. He had drained it considerably. 'Yes, I will.' He smashed the bottle on the road. I ran instinctively to my gate and Sumer followed, laughing.

'Idiot!' I hissed as I panted and tried jumping over the boundary wall. Sumer stopped me from doing that.

'Thanks for being there, Tanie. You're family. Probably greater than that,' he whispered into my neck.

I patted his head. 'I'll always be there for you, Sumer.' We broke the embrace and I turned to climb over the wall.

'Tanie?' he said, as he pushed me.

'Hmmm?'

'Life is going to be terrible from now on. I'll be another reluctant engineer. Are you still willing to flash your tits?'

'No, Sumer.'

'Okay then. Goodnight.'

'Goodnight, Sumer.'

He smiled. She smiled. Problem solved.

The summer went by as the drama of choosing streams, changing schools and starting class eleven unfolded. Autumn came and went. Life continued to troll us and we happily got trolled. Sumer's dad kept a distant eye on his academic integrity, regularly checking in on his tuition test scores and his attendance. He even returned Sumer's camera after Sumer actually scored well on a chemistry test in November.

Not like Sumer suddenly had grown an erection of fondness

for science. His plan was simple—build his father's hopes, play along and then next year, crash his world and smile.

I tried dissuading him from doing so, but then gave up. I was his best friend and I was supposed to support him, come what may.

That winter my dog Liaka died. She was old. But I wasn't ready to let her go. I cried and howled, and how. Sumer was there by my side, unfailingly. Even if it called for bunking his tuitions and missing his assignments. His father came back home around the same time and caught him red-handed, as we once crossed paths with Uncle at the DVD store. We had gone there to get the DVD of *Marley and Me*. Sumer got grounded in the bargain but made sure I set free the pain of losing Liaka.

2012 started. We entered class twelve. I continued to sulk over a life with no love and no dog and Sumer over his physics, chemistry and maths. The handful of 'not-so-pretty-but-bearable-after-a-few-drinks-non-med-girls' in his tuitions kept him from committing suicide.

'I've become a pro at picking the best out of waste,' he would state chauvinistically while I shot him a feminist glance every time he dated a new girl.

The year went on. Then sometime in November, just before the pre-Boards were about to begin, Shiven turned legal. And F Bar opened in Chandigarh. When people started flooding Facebook with their F Bar pictures, the entire gang called for an emergency intervention and decided we couldn't fossilize our lives anymore. Shiven, who had conveniently avoided giving us a birthday treat, was targeted. We needed to rejuvenate our lives with a badass shot in our asses. So we made a Viagra of a plan.

That Saturday night was crazy. And by the end of it, Sumer and I once again lost our friendship.

Well, almost.

'Fuck,' I said, startled, as I dropped my Blackberry, which I was holding in one hand, after it suddenly started to buzz, making the gloss I was applying with the other hand run askew. I carefully bent down in the halter dress I had secretly bought and picked up my phone. 'Sumer's coming to pick us up in ten minutes. He's managed to sneak his car out!' I announced.

'Shhhhh!' Megha hissed. 'For all you know, my mom's still got her ear stuck to the door.'

'Really, now? At 11.30 p.m.?' I whispered in a mocking tone.

'I'm not joking. She looked at me so suspiciously when I told her that you both were coming over for a sleepover, like she knew I was lying.'

'Really?' Stuti's eyes grew big with apprehension.

I quickly put my arm around her. 'Megha told her mom we were coming for a sleepover, and that's exactly what we're going to do…eventually. Sleep. Over. At her house.' The worry on Stuti's face already melting, I continued, 'Going out with the gang for Shiven's "little" birthday celebration to F Bar is just an extra piece of information. It's like filtering the truth.'

'And look at all this.' Megha picked up the bunch of chick flicks she had bought to add authenticity to our sleepover plans. '*Gossip Girl, The Ugly Truth, The Notebook.*' All of these spelled cheese. And romance. And tissue boxes. Everything stereotypically associated with three seventeen-year-old girls spending the night together.

Stuti smiled comfortably again.

'Okay ladies, now quickly, I need a new picture for my BBM.'

We stood together excitedly in front of the mirror. Stuti stood on my left, leaning to one side, one hand on her waist. Megha stood on the other, pouting, her eyes narrowed into dramatic slits. And since both of them had covered all the options available for a socially acceptable, carefully manicured photo that is taken especially in front of the mirror, I chose the grand weapon. I raised my shoulders, bent forward a little, tilted my head and sucked in my cheeks. Just as we were about to click, my phone buzzed again. We sighed.

'Sumer, when was the last time you weren't responsible for something going wrong in my life?'

'Jesus. You really are frustrated. We so need to get you some action tonight. Now come quickly, Viraaj, Shiven and his cousin are already waiting outside the club. And oh, Tanie…I have a surprise for you.'

'He's outside,' I repeated to the others. I skipped the 'something special' bit, thinking it was one of his perverted lines.

Megha quickly put *The Notebook* into the DVD player. I made the beds. Stuti just watched. We surreptitiously reached the front door and just as Megha unlocked it with the duplicate key she had got made, my phone buzzed again and the noise echoed in her silent auditorium of a house. Everyone froze. I hurriedly cut the call.

'Sumerrr,' I groaned under my breath.

Megha and Stuti turned around slowly. Scared to the bases of their butt cracks. Luckily no door opened, no light was switched on. The parents continued to snore. We got out of the house. I swiftly wore my pumps and begun to walk towards Sumer's Endeavour. Behind me, Megha helped Stuti get into her stilettoes. By habit, I walked up to the front passenger seat. It was mine. It had been for the last two years and no one could take it. Not when Sumer was driving. There was no 'shotgun' or 'dibs' on this one. I opened the door.

'Sumer Singh Dhillon, if I could, I would burn your flaccid hairy balls on a simmering flame and eat nachos with extra cheese while I watch you whimper in pain, begging for mercy and—' I froze. The front passenger seat was already occupied. By a fair tall girl with a pretty face, full tits and goddamn amazing legs. Yes, I scanned her completely in that one quick look. She smiled at me, amused, her white teeth complementing her white dress.

'Shanaya, this is my uncouth, uncivilized, insolent, ill-mannered, discourteous and extremely kinky best friend, Tanie.'

Sumer winked at me. I threw a cold-blooded, murderous look at him in response.

'Ignore him,' Shanaya said.

'I've been trying to do that for two years now,' I smiled at her.

'I've been trying to do that for the last six years now,' she replied.

My smile died. Instantly. And I felt paranoid all of a sudden. Before I could rationalize my mood change, Megha tapped me on my shoulder, wondering why I hadn't gotten into the car yet. Stuti, meanwhile, got in from the other side, sitting behind Sumer. Polite introductions were made again. Round three of introductions happened with Megha. And this time he explained why this hot, pretty girl was sitting in my seat.

'Shanaya's dad and Vikram, I mean my father—' Shanaya giggled at this, 'are childhood buddies. She was holidaying with her parents in Shimla and they missed their flight back to Mumbai from Chandigarh this evening. So they're spending the night at our place and since I had plans, I took the liberty of inviting her as well. She's finishing college, in the US.'

Shanaya turned around and spoke to no one in particular. 'I hope you guys don't mind. When Sumer told me that all of you were planning to sneak out and go clubbing, I was like, dude, that's so retro...we did it when we were in ninth grade! I felt so nostalgic.'

I wasn't sure if she was being candid or sarcastic.

'Not at all,' Stuti smiled genuinely.

Shanaya smiled back and spoke to Megha this time. 'By the way, I love the body mist you're wearing. Victoria's Secret, peach-flavoured, right?'

Megha beamed. I choked. For some unexplainable reason, I felt like getting out of the car right then. As if reading my mind, Sumer stepped on the accelerator and the car sped off before I could do anything.

We reached F Bar in ten minutes. This, after Sumer took the longer route, dodging all possible police patrolling barricades. You can host an all-night cricket match on Chandigarh roads, they are that empty at night. Sumer stopped his car at the valet service. He got out immediately and opened the door for Shanaya, and escorted her as the valet boy opened the door for me and I got out with Stuti and Megha. Stuti merrily walked ahead and caught up with them. Megha and I chose to walk slowly. We had just met a bitch. And we needed to tell each other that.

'This woman—'

'This woman—'

We both giggled.

'You know what Sumer is trying to do, right?' Megha asked me.

'Yes. He's trying to act cool so that he can get lucky.'

'No, idiot, he's trying to make you jealous,' she said.

'Me, jealous? Ha! Why?'

She stopped me, turned me around, held me by the shoulders and looked into my eyes. 'Because Tanie…'

'Because, Megha?'

'Because Tanie…'

'What's with the dramatic pauses?'

'Forget it.' She shot me a funny smile and walked on.

'Whatever,' I muttered.

We caught up with everyone. Shiven. Viraaj. Sumer. Random guy whose name I did not know. All the boys had dressed carefully to look like men. Well-fitted shirts. Tucked in. Creased trousers. Pointed leather shoes. Expensive belts. Spicy cologne. Like all of them went for a shopping trip together. So macho.

'You look so...pretty.' Shiven and Megha shared an awkward hug. She turned beetroot-red.

'Okay, everyone get into pairs. Girls, give the bouncer at the gate your sluttiest look. Boys, suck it in, square your shoulders and speak with extra gravity, if spoken to,' Sumer instructed. 'They might ask for ID at the gate. Not all of us are legal yet...just look your eldest best...it works, trust me.' He winked at Shanaya.

I puked internally. Instantly the couples paired up. Shiven conveniently went and stood next to Megha. Stuti bounced to Viraaj. I walked up to my obvious choice, Sumer...and just as I was about to hold his hand, Shanaya came and slid her arm into his from the other side. Now this was getting personal. I looked at Sumer, waiting for him to acknowledge me. Instead, he continued to talk to Shanaya, forgetting me. Completely.

'Tanie. Walk Rohan in,' Shiven said quickly, as he led everyone to the entrance.

I looked at the random guy, who winked at me. Creep.

'Hey. Myself Rohaan.'

He had a fake accent. Like the ones you pick up at the airport or the call centre. I gave him a cursory look. He extended his arm. A part of me died as I slid my arm through it.

We entered the club easily. No ID check. No bribery. Not even the desperate need to throw around the names of contacts and beckon some, if there were any. It was a new club. Either they were lazy with their security or welcomed snooty-looking kids, who would guarantee them a good bill.

Like always, we went dutch on the entry charges. Shiven had promised to take care of the liquor bill. We cruised past the crowd, got used to the dim lighting and the blasting music, and finally reached an area where we weren't unintentionally grinding against sweaty drunk bodies. Drinks were ordered. And chugged. Shots were called for. And drained. We had been drinking for a year now and our capacity showed. Yet I maintained sufficient restraint, learning from my history with birthdays and clubs.

Photos started to get clicked. Megha announced that she needed to go to the washroom. Shiven immediately volunteered to take her. Expensive alcohol was ordered as soon as Shiven was out of sight. When the host is away, the drunk friends will play. Once everyone was done with two more rounds of Jägerbomb shots, Stuti announced loudly that she wanted to dance. Viraaj held her by the waist as they made their way to the dance floor, leaving Sumer, Shanaya, random-creepy-guy-with-a-fake-accent and me behind.

I walked over to Sumer, holding the same bottle of beer that I had been sipping on for the past fifteen minutes. He hadn't left Shanaya's side, or his glass, ever since we had entered the club.

'They're so hooking up tonight!' I shouted in Sumer's ear.

'So am I.' Sumer pointed blatantly towards Shanaya, who was busy texting.

I looked at him carefully. Vacant eyes. Goofy smile. I snatched his glass and smelled it. 'You're drinking whisky? You're supposed to drive us back!'

He freed himself from my grip. 'Tanie. Stop being so uptight, okay? I've had enough of your whining.' He burped. More gaseous proof of all the alcohol he had guzzled. 'Just because you're fucking single doesn't mean I can't get some action. And it's not whisky. It's Scotch.'

He was drunk. And being mean. And honest. I showed him

the finger. He simply turned around, walked over to Shanaya, took her phone away with one hand, slid the other around her waist and got lost in the crowd with her. I picked up Shiven's unfinished glass of whisky and chugged it down. Still pissed and angry at what Sumer had said, I quickly drank the leftover beer in Stuti's bottle as well. I saw a stray vodka shot on the table and went for it. Without lime and salt. YUCK. My stomach revolted after the sudden assault. I instantly got a kick.

'Seems like it's just the two of us now.' Random creepy guy, who had been lurking around, came up to me.

My head spun and I saw two of him. I used both my hands and showed him both my fingers. He dissolved away from sight immediately. I took a few careful deep breaths. Waited for a couple of minutes for someone less random, like Stuti, Megha or that ass Sumer, to come back and realize I was beyond the level of comfortable drunk. No one came. I called Megha. She continued to answer Shiven's booty call, ignoring me. I texted Stuti. Who, even when sober, doesn't realize when her phone is buzzing. Even though I did not want to, I pressed 2 on the speed dial, calling Sumer. It went unanswered.

Perhaps it was the sudden inflow of different types of alcohol. Perhaps it was the happy drunk people around me. Perhaps it was the sad reality of what Sumer had said in jest. Perhaps it was because nobody answered my calls. But right there, right then, standing all by myself in the club, emotion engulfed me and I suddenly felt lonelier than ever. My eyes welled up. I blinked them hard to fight back the tears. And just then, HE walked up to me.

'Hi,' he shot me a lopsided grin. Like he hadn't hurt me at all.

I looked away. He couldn't know that I was crying.

Taking a step forward, he bent down to come near my face. He reeked of Scotch.

'Tan...Tan,' he sang, 'is that really you? Why didn't I notice you earlier? You look so hot.'

'Just go...go away.'

He smirked. 'Why? Are you still angry with me? C'mon. Shit happens. I screwed up, okay? Come, let's get a drink and talk this out. You know I love you.'

Those words. And I melted. In an instant. He came really close to me. I could feel his breath on my face. His hands went around me. His lips traversing the distance. I closed my eyes. Parted my lips. And then...

'Don't you dare, you SON OF A BITCH.'

Sumer had come up and pushed Rehaan away from me.

That's the problem with heartbreak. You never move on. You just move ahead. Everyone thinks they are healing. That time will make them forget it all. They all have different speeds. Some crawl. Some brisk-walk. Some jog. Some dash. Some fly. Out of it. And just when you feel you're ready to believe again, a stray song, a distant image, a random moment or that person comes back into your life and makes you realize that with heartbreak, you never move on, you just move ahead.

'Shhh, Tanie, it's okay.'

I continued to cry into Sumer's shirt.

'Tanie, stop now, please.' He stroked my hair gently.

We were sitting on the steps leading to the service staff entry to F Bar. After Sumer had pushed Rehaan away, he had simply smirked and walked off. Sumer was about to go after him but he had stopped, seeing me shivering uncontrollably. He had put his arm around me and walked me out of the club. To somewhere more quiet.

'Tanie, can I ask you something?' Sumer said solemnly.

I sniffled in response.

'When Megha sat in the car…umm…her perfume…didn't it smell like…ummm…'

'Car freshener?' I added.

'Yes! Just that. Wonder why she would use it?'

I smiled feebly and lifted my head to face him. 'All this time I thought I was over him, but I'm clearly not.'

'It's okay. I'm sure you'll feel much better tomorrow morning,' he tried to reassure me, continuing to look into my eyes.

I retaliated with a contrasting passion. 'I…I won't be able to ever fall in love again. I was so affected by seeing him inside. After he cheated on me!' I pointed my finger at my chest to emphasize. 'I can't believe this, Sumer…I was about to kiss him back! After all that he did to me! How could I—'

Sumer stopped me from speaking any further. His lips skimmed over mine. A moment into the kiss, he pulled away. I was too stunned to react.

'Did you think about him when I kissed you right now?' Sumer asked as he edged back. Anticipating the worst.

'What the—' I began, but he interjected.

'Just answer my question, did you think about him, when I kissed you this time?'

'What…Fuc—'

'Stop swearing and just answer my question, did you think about him when I kissed you this time?'

I thought about it. Hard. 'No,' I found myself blurting.

His eyebrows shot up. 'So you're clearly over him and can trust in love and people again. You cannot not trust people. We all place our trust in the wrong person, sometime in life. It's like buying a pair of jeans. They look good from a distance. You try them on, they fit you perfectly but as time flies, they start to bring you discomfort and you finally throw them away. But then you go back and buy new jeans, don't you? Why? Because you can't possibly do without them. Trust is that pair of jeans, Tanie.'

He made no sense. Yet for some strange reason, I smiled. Then laughed. Uncontrollably. 'You're fucking awesome.' I hugged him.

He broke the embrace. 'It may hurt to look back and you might be afraid of looking ahead, but I can promise you one thing, Tanie Brar, that I'm here for you... Right now and forever.'

We both continued to look into each other's eyes. His cell phone rang, breaking the moment.

'Is it Shanaya?' I winked at him.

He ignored it. 'Let's go inside now, we need to collect everyone and leave. It's already 1 a.m. and you girls have conveniently forgotten you're out on a sneak. And if Vikram finds out that I'm out with his car and his friend's daughter...' He got up and gave me a hand.

We walked back. Just as we were about to enter the club again, I stopped him. 'Sumer, I'm sorry.'

'You should be,' pat came the reply.

'Hell, why?' I asked, surprised.

'You cock-blocked me, Tanie. She's going back tomorrow morning.'

'But you got to kiss me.'

'Well...'

'Well...'

He smiled. She smiled. Problem solved.

You may accidentally belong to Einstein's gene pool. You may be Zuckerberg's sperm. You may be Clinton's child. But when it comes to getting into the college of your choice, here, in India, one March decides the march of your life.

The twelfth-grade Board exams took place in the March of 2013. Everyone—Stuti, Megha, Shiven, Viraaj and I—went on a royally bad trip. None of us, barring Stuti, were the type who could cram books and puke it all out on the recycled sheets of paper CBSE provided us with. The country's education system seriously needed a revolution. *Three Idiots* had released four years ago and become a blockbuster, but that clearly hadn't changed much.

Sumer was the least bothered. This was his time to get back at his father. The Boards ended. Somehow. I hardly met Sumer during April. Kapil Sibal hadn't yet had a divine intervention and for non-medical students, the real battle began once the Boards ended.

Sumer's life was hostage to his father's stern and expectant eye and a combination of life-threatening syllables. IIT-JEE. AIEEE. BITS. SET. SNAP. He had a trillion entrance exams to take and fuck up.

'He questions me if I spend more than thirty minutes in the toilet, Tanie! What else do I do to vent my stress? Anyway, I don't give a fuck about the results. We're so doing this tomorrow. He needs to know that I don't want to do goddamn engineering,' Sumer said on the phone, the night before our Board results were to be declared.

I was shitting bricks myself. At any cost, I had to get away from home and live. Fall in love with a hot guy again. Get in a serious relationship with him. Make out with him at India Gate. Okay, maybe not that. Get a secret tattoo of our initials, which would give Mom a mini heart attack when she found out later. If she ever did. And have a few decently wild experiences that I could tell my grandchildren about.

But all of this could only happen if I left home. There was

no chance in hell I was staying in Chandigarh for college and living with my parents. No, they weren't bad people. They were just good parents. And that's where the problem lay. They were reasonably approachable. Open to discussion. And often let me be. They weren't the type who would switch off the Wi-Fi router at night or randomly walk into my room and take away my cell phone. But then again, they weren't raised in hippie Goa. They still thought I was too young to date. Or indulge. In alcohol. Sex. Drugs. They had green-lit Delhi, but nothing beyond that. That also only if I got admission in a good DU college, which effectively meant that I had to get a way above decent aggregate and getting that, to put it simply, was as likely as betting on Sumer getting through IIT Delhi.

The sun came out early on the morning of 28 May. Mom and Aarti aunty came back from the temple with tikas on their foreheads and prasad in their hands. Dad didn't go to play golf. Sumer's father went about his usual yoga routine and walked in at 9 a.m., followed by Sumer.

So the plan was simple. We would check our results together. And when Sumer's father threw a fit over his result, Sumer would stand up to him for the last two years.

We were so not confident about our plan.

We went online. I checked my results first. Fed in my roll number, closed my eyes and pressed enter. There were shrieks. Gasps. Squeals. And then Sumer hugged me. An aggregate of 91 per cent in the best of four subjects. I had no clue how, but yes, that was my marksheet. English Honours, not at St Stephen's but Lady Shri Ram (nope, I wasn't going to an all-girls' college) or Hindu (yes! That for sure).

You know the feeling when you've been constipated for days and you take a classic dump? Yes, that's just how I felt. Orgasmic. It was short-lived, though.

'Sumer. Type in your roll number,' his father ordered.

Sumer obeyed. His father towered over him. Just before Sumer pressed enter, we connected. Our eyes. The wavelength. The vibe. We had to do this. Now. My heart sank. I knew what was coming. I just hadn't expected it to be this bad.

'58 per cent! HOW COULD YOU GET A 40 IN MATHEMATICS!' The sound of the slap blasted in our living room. A grave silence followed.

And then Sumer spoke, softly yet firmly. 'I don't want to do engineering, Dad. I hope you understand now.'

His father raised his hand again.

'STOP!' I yelled.

He stopped midway. My parents, Sumer, his parents—all stood there appalled.

'Uncle, you have no right to do this,' I spewed.

'Stay out of this, Tanie,' his father said through gritted teeth.

'But—'

Mom held me back. Sumer's father stomped out of our house. His mother, embarrassed by her husband more than her son, who she knew had no heart to do what he was being asked to, grabbed Sumer by his hand and followed.

That morning my dream came true and my best friend's nightmare began. A tear rolled down my cheek.

Sumer: last seen today at 8:47 p.m.
Tanie Are you okay?!   10:00 p.m.
Tanie Call/Message ASAP!   10:02 p.m.
Tanie Pick up your phone. Mom won't let me come to your house.   10:45 p.m.
Sumer: last seen yesterday at 8:47 p.m.
Tanie Sumer. Pick up the landline.   4:41 p.m.
Tanie Sumer… If you reply, I'll send you an up-skirt picture.   5:34 p.m.
Sumer: last seen yesterday at 8:47 p.m.
Tanie   6:49 p.m. Status Marks don't make you awesome. I have an awesome best friend.
Sumer: last seen yesterday at 8:47 p.m.

'Why aren't you ready yet?' Mom entered my room later that night.

Dad had made a reservation at my favourite restaurant to celebrate my result. I did not reply. She sat on the edge of my bed and took my hand in hers. I immediately withdrew it. I was still mad at her for not letting me go to Sumer's house.

'Tanie, every parent wants the best for their child,' she explained.

'So they slap their children in public if they don't do well in something they did not want to do in the first place?' I snapped back.

She did not lose her patience. Damn these parents.

'It's their personal matter, Tanie. I know he's your best friend and you're feeling bad for him. But I hope you're also concerned about your parents' feelings and will dress up and come down. For our happiness.' At the door, she spoke again, 'I hope we matter also, Tanie.' She left.

'UGH!' I shouted as I got up to change. We went for dinner. My parents and my body. My mind wandered elsewhere. We came back. I again checked my phone, Facebook and WhatsApp. I checked with the gang. He hadn't replied to anyone. I tried to sleep. Unsuccessfully. Then at around 3 a.m., I saw a red laser beam of light being flashed at my window. The kind that people use in theatres and auditoriums to fool around. I sprang out of bed and opened the window. Sumer stood at his window, frantically waving his hands. I tried to decipher what he was trying to say. He was pointing at something. I narrowed my eyes to concentrate and finally realized that he was asking me to come down, out onto the road.

'Don't have the keys to the main gate,' I tried to signal him.

'What?' he signalled back.

I tried again. He did not get it. I got my phone, signalled him to call or message. He showed me a thumbs down. Idea! I decided to use dumb-charade gestures. After a few tries he got what I was trying to do. Five words. English. First word—I. He got it instantly. Second—No. He got it in the second try. Third—Keys. He didn't get it. I ran and got a pair of keys. He finally got it. I pointed to the main gate then. Phew. It was his turn to act. I concentrated and got the first three words in no time. Jump. Gate. Your. I got stuck on the fourth one. He turned around to show me his ass and then growled like a lion and pointed at my house.

'Gan...lion...sher...gan...sher...house...den...GARDEN!' I smiled, signalled a thumbs up, stealthily tiptoed to Mom and Dad's room, heard their peaceful snoring, dashed through the house to the kitchen, almost tripped over maid who slept on the floor there, unlatched the kitchen door and went out into the backyard.

Sumer came after a couple of minutes. I hugged him. 'WHY WEREN'T—' I began excitedly. He covered my mouth with his hand. He was grounded and so would I be if Mom and Dad found out I was out in the garden with him, at this hour. We sat on the grass.

'Why didn't you reply to my messages? I even offered to flash,' I whispered.

'Vikram had my phone.'

'Oops.' We both smiled.

'Don't worry, I have a password on it.'

'Are you all right?'

'Oh, I'm perfect. My father slapped me. I'm officially grounded till the results of the entrance exams come out. And I know I'm not going to do any better in them. Also, I have no clue about what I'm going to do with my life,' he said with a straight face.

I slapped him on the same cheek as his father had.

'Aow!'

'Sorry. Does it still hurt?'

'A little. Okay, now listen.' He took my hand and thrust an envelope into it.

'What's this?'

'My suicide note. I want you to proofread it, Miss Writer.'

I ignored him and opened the envelope. I switched on the torch in my mobile and read the letter loudly enough for the two of us to hear.

'*Dear Sumer S. Dhillon,*

Congratulations! You have been accepted to the Singapore Film School, with a 50 per cent scholarship for tuition and boarding.' I paused.

'Read on!' Sumer nudged me.

'*Please be advised that this scholarship holds true only in the event of you securing at least 75 per cent in the non-sciences stream and 55 per cent in the science stream.*'

I did not need to read further.

'I had applied to this film school, sending them a detailed account of all the amateur movies that I had made, the certificates I had for everything, from debating to state-level basketball to my social work, etc. And I told them how I was being made to do non-medical and needed a college with a vision such as theirs to support my dream. I nailed the statement of purpose. It was so cheesy. And karmic as it is, their provisional acceptance letter came today. Luckily Shanti received it before my parents could see it. It's not a great film school, but it's a film school at least.'

I gasped in disbelief.

'Don't get mad that I didn't tell you about this, Tanie. I randomly applied to them in January. Just while I was surfing the net, their school's ad popped up. I didn't even think they'd reply. But they did. And how. They've sent me a conditional acceptance letter, and my scores fulfil their criteria, so I'm eligible to enrol with them.'

'Yes, I'm mad at you for keeping such a big secret from me, but that's not the point, Sumer. First, I don't think Uncle is going to take this lightly. Also, it's just a 50 per cent scholarship, what about the rest? We're talking about Singapore. It's kind of expensive.' I had once Googled a list of film schools with him. And we both knew they charged a bomb.

'If Dad doesn't agree, I'm going to steal money from home and run away. I know Mom won't judge me.' His tone reeked of business.

'Are you insane?'

'Or I'll ask my mama. Or my nana and nani, they're loaded.'

'You know you're talking about lakhs here, right?' I questioned, cautiously.

'Yes,' he nodded. 'I'm still obviously hoping that Dad understands, though. You know how much filmmaking means to me.'

I understood everything. I had seen him go mad with the camera when we went to Sukhna Lake for early morning jogs. He would capture the lake, the birds, the people, all so beautifully and then work wonders with his footage using some software on his MacBook.

Sumer looked at his watch.

'Vikram gets up at four to fart, let's leave,' he grinned.

We got up and brushed our bums with our hands.

'Thanks for being there,' he said.

'You too, Dhillon,' I replied.

'And for not wearing a bra at night.'

I shot him a disgusted look. He pulled me towards him and gave me the fuzziest hug ever.

He cleared his throat. 'Tanie, I know if this happens, I'll be in Singapore and you in Delhi, and even if the distance separates us, I'll always be there for you.'

Emotion choked my voice. 'That was…so…gay.'

'I know. And I love you, Tan Tan.'
'I love you too, Dhillon.'
He smiled. She smiled. Problem solved.

I waited impatiently to hear from Sumer the next day but he never called or replied to any of the Facebook messages I sent him. His WhatsApp status showed that his phone was still with Uncle. The same cycle of anxiousness carried into the next day. And the day after that. Finally, the entire gang landed up at his house, at my insistence. If mutiny was the answer to freeing him from the clutches of his father, I needed the soldiers.

'Sumer's gone to his grandparents' house in Mumbai,' Aarti aunty told us, without even a trace of her characteristic excitement, as she opened the door.

'Oh. When? How? Why? What's his number there? When is he coming back?' The questions darted at her. I think we scared her.

'He's not carrying his mobile. I'll tell him to call you.'

The door shut. We all left, confused.

Two days later, he messaged on Facebook: *'Continuing with engineering. I'll be in Mumbai for some time. Don't know when I'll be back exactly. Getting a local number soon.'*

I messaged him back immediately, asking him to call me. He saw the message but did not reply. That night, when I was tossing in bed, in confusion, he called me very briefly to tell me his film school plan had tanked. And that he would call me again soon. The next morning, I got a curt, emotionless call from him, informing me that he hadn't cleared IIT-JEE. The next time he called was when the AIEEE results came out. This time he told me that his father was figuring out a college for him. Where? He didn't know himself.

All our subsequent correspondences were erratic and mechanical.

The morning I told my parents that I was choosing Hindu over LSR, Aarti aunty and Uncle also left for Mumbai. Mom threw a fit. Dad poured himself another glass of whisky and I continued to rant as I tried to make them understand why I wanted to go to Hindu rather than LSR. Them being parents, they could never understand how emotionally, physically and psychologically damaging the thought of spending the three most important years of my life with depressing shots of just estrogen around me could be. I finally won.

Everyone else also began the next chapter in their lives. Megha was accepted by a random college in New York, which was just about what she aspired for. Viraaj decided to go to Mumbai to join an acting school. Stuti, despite scoring the highest in our gang, settled for a BCom from MCM, an all girls' college in Chandigarh. Her parents wouldn't let her leave the city. And would probably get her married off as soon as college ended. Shiven decided to go to London.

Even as July started, nobody, including me, knew where Sumer would end up. Or when he would come back.

We all got our answer at Shiven's farewell party.

July was officially the month of farewells, goodbyes and promises.

We actually thought we'd all never separate, come what may. What we didn't realize at that time was that these promises would eventually break, as everyone would get busy with their new college lives. In different cities. Countries. Time zones. With different friends. Priorities. And lifestyles.

No one at that time knew that staying in touch wasn't going to last beyond a couple of weeks, with just birthdays and breakups being the times when we would call each other. Or when we came back home in the summers and got together. Living through it like there was no distance between us and then separating like we never met. Yes, we would regularly like each other's pictures on Facebook, but that would just be about obligatory clicks on the laptop's keypad. Yes, we would randomly drunk text each other, but those smiles would die with the hangover the next morning.

Shiven was leaving for London the next day. So that night his parents had left the house and their unattended bar to him and his friends. Though he had called several other people who were scattered through the house in comfortable corners, washrooms and his backyard where the main party was supposed to be, we all retired with six beer bottles to the intimate comfort of Shiven's room. And Shiven himself came along with us. Sumer hadn't yet come back from Mumbai. His absence hijacked the conversation.

'Not being homo here, but I don't like the fact that I won't get to see him before I leave.' Shiven took a sip from his beer bottle. Everyone nodded in unison.

'Tanie, any news on his admission front?' Megha asked.

'Nope.'

Shiven saw me look at his hand clasped with Megha's and smiled. Proud, not embarrassed. Two years ago they had hooked up over alcohol. This morning they had broken up over coffee. They never named their relationship. They just lived it. They chose to let go of each other, perhaps not because they liked each other but because they loved each other. And they knew handling the distance right now would kill the love.

'So this is where the orgy is happening. Good I'm not wearing any underwear,' the door opened and a very familiar voice boomed.

'SUMER!' Shrieks, gasps and friendly abuses all crashed

into each other. I dashed to him and pinned him down with my hug.

'Wow. So eager, Tanie. I like the intensity.'

'Fuck you.'

We got up. He met everyone. Bear hugs. Butt slaps. High fives. And an array of exquisite abuses hurled at him. He took it all sportingly. It was only once he sat down with a beer bottle that I realized that he looked like he had dropped a couple of kilos. And his eyes were sort of red and vacant. Like they were tired of crying. Or deprived of sleep. Or he simply hadn't removed his lenses for a few days. Eventually the excitement died and gave birth to an awkward silence. The spotlight was on him.

'What?' He shrugged.

'So...when did you come back?' I initiated the conversation for everyone.

'I landed an hour ago and came here directly.'

Awkward silence again.

'And...?' I continued

'And what? Mumbai's a good city. I met Shanaya.' He smiled. But it didn't reach his eyes.

'What's up on the college front?' Viraaj directly asked him.

'Oh, that.' He held my gaze. 'Believe it or not, I got admission in this random college in Pune for civil engineering, through the sports quota, but Dad wants me to do mechanical engineering.' He smiled awkwardly. 'So he managed to get me a back-door entry in BM Solanki College in Gurgaon. It's a pretty neat college.' He beamed. No one else did, though.

'Guys, I'm okay with this. Trust me.' He playfully put his arm around my neck and choked me. 'At least I get to be with Tanie... And the sweetest part is, Dad has agreed to let me stay at our old house in Gurgaon—a 2BHK, all to myself! Also, who says I can't make movies alongside? Nobody studies in engineering anyway.' He ruffled my hair.

'Cheers to that, then,' Viraaj said.

Everyone raised their bottles. And Sumer gulped down his beer in one go.

Sumer drank a lot that evening and though he kept cracking jokes, dodging the obvious questions with his wit and sarcasm and being his drunk merry self, a part of me knew.

It's funny how nobody notices that people often raise a solitary toast to happiness and down a bottle to despair.

Sumer was in pain. I realized that when I dragged him to the washroom and he puked into the pot for the third time.

'Sumer, careful!' I pulled him up as he almost dunked his head into the pot. I quickly locked the bathroom door. Made Sumer sit on the stool near the shower. Got a towel and cleaned him up. I went to wash my hands and turned around to see Sumer stretched out on the toilet floor, swimming. I tried to pick him up but he fell down again. He smiled dreamily, unaffected by the painful fall.

'SUMER!' I held him by his collar and shook him.

'What's happeningggg insiiiiide?' Viraaj sang. I heard laughter from outside. Sumer also laughed.

'Just in case, Sumer, there's a rubber on the second shelf.' More drunk laughter.

I ignored them.

'Tanie...come...let's swimm...we're going to the same city for...collleeege.' He started to laugh uncontrollably.

I got irritated. 'Just come out on your own.' I was about to unlock the door when he spoke, in the tiniest voice ever.

'Vikram isn't my father.'

The regular rant. My hand went to the knob.

'He's my mother's second husband.'

The hairs on the nape of my neck stood up. I walked back to him slowly. Shiny beads of a broken secret, held for so long, streamed out of his eyes, like they had had enough, guarding a pain that needed to be shared. He hugged me.

'Tanie...' he whispered into my ear. 'He's not my father. My biological father cheated on my mother and they got separated when I was three years old.' He hugged me tighter as he shivered. 'I found out...' he hiccupped, 'about this...when I showed him the film school offer letter... I was never supposed to know this...it came out in anger...that's why I went to Mumbai...I just couldn't handle this... He's kept my mother happy, Tanie...he gave her everything. I...I can't be so selfish... Engineering...that's all that he wants me to do.'

I tried to comfort him. Processing each word that had come out of his mouth. Everything suddenly made sense.

'Promise me you won't tell anyone this.' His voice choked with tears.

'I won't, Sumer.'

He wanted to puke again. I helped him. Once he was done, I made him sit on the pot. Drunk, he kept cleaning a clean spot on his pants with a hand towel, ignoring the soiled patch completely. I looked on fondly.

'Tanie, I love my mom, more than I love anyone in this world... And if this makes her happy...I'll be happy with this. It's four years of engineering...I'll just do filmmaking later...' He rested his head against the wall and continued, 'Anyhow, an unsuccessful engineer is the stamp card you need to enter any creative field.' He grinned.

That's where you draw a line between a rebel and a fanatic. A fanatic takes decisions. A rebel makes choices. A fanatic lives by his decision. A rebel sticks to a choice till he believes it's his own. In that moment, I knew Sumer had made the choice to accept everything he had stood against. And he was going to stick by his new choice. Filmmaking was his choice then. Engineering was going to be his choice now.

I extended my arms, signalling to him to hold them and get up. We had to get out of the washroom. The world outside, figuratively and literally, would never understand that two drunk friends, locked inside a washroom, could come out stronger, baring everything but their bodies to each other. He held my hand, got up and pulled me into a hug.

'I'm with you in whatever you do or choose to do, Sumer.' He didn't reply. 'Sumer?' I rubbed his back. He had passed out, hugging me. I broke the embrace carefully, making sure he didn't fall down. I looked at him. Maybe it was the alcohol. Maybe it was the emotion. Or maybe it just felt right. I kissed him. Very briefly.

'Tanie, Sumer…What ARE you guys up to?' Megha giggled from the other side of the door.

'Making sure we stay best friends.'

Sumer opened his bloodshot eyes, still drunk out of his mind.

He smiled. She smiled. Problem solved.

'C'mon…you can do it,' Sumer insisted.

I swallowed a lump of apprehension. Gathered my breath. Instructed my heart to not pound so hard. It was the first time I was doing something like this. 'I…I'm scared,' I whispered, uncomfortable with the position.

'Tanie…you've already gone half the distance, just close your eyes and go for it! I promise, I'll hold you tight. It won't hurt.' He extended his arms as he reassured me.

It was dark, the silence of the night adding dauntingly to what was happening. I looked at him. His eager eyes. The crooked smile plastered on his face. Like this was everything he wanted.

'I can't, Sumer. I'm sorry.'

'C'mon, Tanie. It's hardly anything. You can come down!'

I carefully raised my hips a little and decided to go for it, but then stopped again.

'Dude, we don't have all night. Now will you!' he shouted this time.

'Quiet!'

'Okay. Sorry. Now…please will you?' he pleaded restlessly.

'Okay. You ready?'

'Yes…'

'Yeah?'

'Yes…go for it.'

I closed my eyes and took the plunge. 'Aaah,' I gasped.

'Wow. You're heavy.'

I had successfully jumped over the tall gate at my paying-guest accommodation in Delhi and landed firmly in Sumer's grip.

Let's put the blame on Hollywood. *American Pie. Van Wilder. Project X. Sorority Wars.* Movies that ushered our generation into our teenage years, mentally and well… Movies that excited us, for reasons best left unmentioned. Movies that painted the picture in our minds that college life was going to be all about abandoning the mundane safety of home and entering an unending after-party with drunken nights, hungover early morning lectures, hazy days spent at pool parties that regularly got busted and fun-filled evenings ending in barbeques gone wrong—all while you struck up lifelong friendships in overcrowded washrooms as people took turns to puke and, most importantly, you accidentally chanced upon the love of your life on a deserted road, in your sweatpants, as you went for your morning jog.

Cut to India, September 2013, two months into Hindu College, Delhi. My life had been like eating cheap Chinese food from the roadside—filling but not fulfilling. For starters, Mom, knowing that I was raring to break the chains of trust she had bound me in, chose a PG for me to stay in on Hudson Road, owned by a menopausal fifty-year-old lady with the night vision of an owl, the agility of a cheetah and a mobile that had my mom's number on speed dial, just in case she saw me return past my 11 p.m. deadline. Then there were the early morning lectures in classes with more girls and only a handful of average boys. And all the cute ones were either taken or gay. Yes, there were a couple of seniors whom you could totally give a second look to but no one had asked me if I liked coffee or beer yet. I had been asked out, though, during the orientation programme, by a dude who had sold his land in the village, bought Armani shades and now proposed to girls inside the auditorium with panache.

Then there were friends—Tanya, Sonya, Amrita, Rishabh, Saraansh—people from college whom I had started to hang out with but wasn't yet friendly enough with to pile on to for uninvited stay-overs at their places. Then again, it had just been two months into college and if I asked Mom for too many nightouts with 'friends' she hardly knew, she would definitely come down to Delhi and give me another of her 'handle-your-freedom-with-care' lectures.

Sumer, on the other hand, was already living it up. With a 2BHK apartment, a full-time cook, a loving mother who believed in supporting him in every way possible now that he was doing what her husband wanted him to, his old crazy friends and a car all to himself, he always had a drunk story to share every time we met.

Not that he loved engineering, but he didn't particularly mind it either. Nope, his wasn't going to be a story about struggles in an IIT that would become a bestselling novel a few years later. Rather, his elitist private engineering college was practically a camping site for bratty, unfocused 'engineers' who didn't want to pursue engineering in the first place.

So when one Friday night we were video calling on Viber, and I casually joked to him that I really felt like sneaking out of the PG, Sumer ignored the casualness in my voice, arrived at my PG and asked me to jump over the gate. We were going to a house party in Defence Colony at one of his friend's places.

'I won't know your friends.'

'You know me and they know me. So you'll get to know them.'

'I'm in my jammies and I can't wear a dress and jump over.'

'Just carry it along. I'll sort a place for you to change.'

'And make-up?'

'You're a pretty girl. You don't need make-up.'

'And what if Aunty finds out?'

'She won't. I'll drop you back early morning. Just tell her you had gone for a jog.'

I had arguments. He had reasons. I had apprehensions. He had answers. The plan sucked balls. But then it was exciting. I gave in.

'So where am I changing?' I questioned for the third time in the last twenty minutes. We had just crossed the Delhi Golf Course. Sumer didn't answer. Instead he increased the volume of the song he was listening to and started to sing along, loudly. A flash of angry realization hit me. I turned down the volume and glared silently at him. He pretended not to notice and went for the music system again. Instinctively, I sank my nails into his hand.

'Oww!' He freed it as he rashly overtook a white Corolla from the wrong side in the same instant. 'You'll get us in an accident, Tanie!'

'You thought I would change in the car?' I had bigger issues to deal with. The Corolla we had overtaken tried to overtake us in turn. But Sumer didn't let it.

Unannounced car racing to men is what sudden gossip sessions are to women. It's about being at the top of your game. All the time.

Sumer slammed the accelerator and started cutting through the late night traffic like a maniac. The Corolla guy was in no mood to take things lying down. He followed close behind. Both cars carved a dangerous serpentine trail as they crossed the Defence Colony flyover. As we got off it, Sumer tried to take a sharp left turn and momentarily lost control. He managed to get the car in control again but ended up getting stuck behind a truck, which wouldn't budge. That was enough for the Corolla guy. He took an even sharper but much better-controlled left turn, squeezing between Sumer's car and the pavement. He finally drew parallel on my side of the car and rolled down the window. It all happened too fast, but I saw him clearly for a moment. And boy, was he hot!

A strong jawline. An intentional three-day stubble, the muscled arm that spoke about his routine with the dumb-bells showing in the short-sleeved T-shirt he was wearing. A tattoo peeking out from under the sleeve. Our eyes locked for a moment. And he smirked, ever so slightly. I felt my cheeks burn. And off he sped, giving a struggling Sumer what he rightly deserved. The finger.

'If you weren't with me, I would have gone after him and fucked his happiness.' Sumer sulked like a true boy.

'But he was hot!' I further tortured his ego.

He continued to sulk as we entered Defence Colony and parked the car a little before his friend's house. It was past midnight and the inactivity in the lane seconded the time.

'No one's around. Please change quickly.' Sumer turned around, picked up a bottle of vodka and a quarter of Old Monk from the back seat and opened the car door.

'What's the booze for?'

'Oh, it's a BYOB thing,' he said as he started to get out of the car.

'BYOB?' I asked, confused.

'Bring your own booze, Tan Tan. Now change, I'll give you cover.'

'You should have told me. I would have brought something too.'

'It's okay,' he snapped at me, still nursing his battered ego.

I inched forward and pulled his cheeks. 'It's okay, Sumer...so what if you lost to that hot guy? You still get to steal a glance at my bra.'

The sullenness on his face evaporated. Instantly. And gave way to a smile. 'Really?'

'No.' I shut the door on his face, got into the back seat and fished out my dress. I quickly looked around at the empty street and then at Sumer, who had settled his butt on the bonnet of the car and was trying really hard to look at his phone. I knew his balls wanted him to stare. But his heart knew the language of care. I quickly took off my top, slid on the dress and then pulled down my shorts. Choking on the body mist Sumer had once stolen from my handbag to replace his Ambi Pure, I got out of the car, wore my pumps, ruffled my hair carefully and walked up to him. He 'who' was still pretending to be busy messaging. I tapped his shoulder. 'Let's go.'

He turned around. And just stood there with his mouth open.

I shut it for him. 'What?'

'Nothing. I thought you caught me watching porn again,' he joked. 'By the way...you...you look amazing.'

'Well thank you, Dhillon, I must add you've been working well on your guns. If only you also went shopping with me for formal shirts. Grow out of your T-shirt phase, please. The last time I saw you wear a formal shirt was at F Bar.'

I held his arm for support as I tottered in the heels and we walked to his friend's house. 'Sumer, whose house are we going to?' I asked as we reached the gate. It was a pretty neat house. Two-storied. A cosy, well-tended garden. Liberal use of glass.

'Oh...Um...' he paused. 'Don't be mad...but...it's Liaka's

house. We got talking again…and her parents were out of town…and she told me to come over. All of my friends were going, so…'

I froze. My first house party in college. At my best friend's ex-girlfriend's house. And the fact that she thinks I was responsible for their break-up.

Dear Life,
Hi, this is when we meet.

Today we will learn about a rarely discussed but widely seen species in the female animal kingdom known as Bitchius Maximus, or more commonly, bitch. This species can exist in extreme climates and is often said to leave a trail of cold despair wherever it resides. For better research purposes, our sample comprises members of the species who are in their biological prime, that is, between the ages of sixteen to twenty-two. There are many ways for the naked eye to observe and identify bitches— the way they look, where they exist, how they behave and why they are the way they are. Pancaked faces, bulimic waistlines, porcelain skin, perfect hair days and taut tits are some of the visual references used to identify them. They thrive on the entire planet, barring Antarctica. At a microscopic level, they thrive in high schools, colleges, offices and places of social interaction, such as clubs and pubs. They are known to come from economically superior families and often exhibit traits such as snobbery, insecurity, mood swings, drama and narcissism. They order mineral water at restaurants, wear over-sized sunglasses, try fitting into clothes from the kids' section and often use a vernacular most commonly used by professionals who drink tea at 3.00 a.m. at call centres. Bitches are known to form the tip of the pyramid in any social structure and to fuel their fragile egos, they always have their less beautiful, less mean, less conniving sidekicks in tow, who work on their orders to weed out 'intelligentia yetus prettius maximus'—another female species that has been at war with them since time immemorial. Bitches exhibit the fine talent of bitching, an art few appreciate and fewer master. A few popular members of this species are Blair Waldorf from *Gossip Girl*, Sharpay Evans from *High School Musical*, Santana Lopez from *Glee*, Clove from *The Hunger Games* and an eighteen-year-old tall, dusky and very attractive fashion student from Delhi, India, called Liaka Malhotra.

It started as soon she met us at the door. Sumer got an intimate hug and I a frigid stare, followed by a contrived smile so cold, it could easily be emailed to Al Gore to solve the problem of global warming. I felt her scan me as she led us upstairs to 'her' floor. She delivered us there and quickly darted to her room. Probably to throw up again.

'Ignore her. She's just—'

'Bitter.'

'It's been two years now.'

'But she clearly still likes you.'

'Well, I like her butt as well. She's the easiest booty call. And she doesn't come with expectations to perform.'

'That I agree with.'

We laughed.

The party wasn't as bad as the introductions had been. The regular crowd—drunk pseudo-intellectuals talking about how much they like alternative music, secretly waiting for '*Chaar Botal Vodka*' to play; stoners with their potent 'stuff' hot-boxing a room and talking about how they should totally do a trip to Parvati Valley in the summer; the paparazzi crowd coming together for selfies one moment and then bitching about each other the next; the couples locked in the washrooms, hiding freshly planted hickeys; the desperados lurking in the shadows; a variable playlist ranging from trance and EDM to commercial Bollywood and Honey Singh, of course. Dim lighting. Fancy scented candles. Bowls of chips with low-fat hung curd dip. A movable bar, where Sumer kept refilling his and my glasses.

I was enjoying the scene completely, on my second glass of vodka and Coke, politely smiling at a joke Sumer's friend was trying really hard to qualify as one, in an obvious attempt at hitting on me, when she rose from the dead.

'THE MIXERS ARE OVER,' Liaka broadcast with an expression graver than KRK's in *Deshdrohi*. The Oscar-worthy performance caught everyone's attention. The music was lowered. And a huddle of drunk people surrounded her.

'WHAT ARE WE GOING TO DO NOW?' The drama continued.

'I don't know if I am capable of producing any of the mixers, Liaka,' Sumer replied loudly, pulling her into his arms.

Everybody laughed. Including me. And Liaka caught onto that.

'But there's so much alcohol left!' she said, snuggling up to him further.

Sumer chugged his drink. He was on his ninth glass now. In our last two years of alcoholic indulgences, we always alternated between the roles of casual drinker and guzzler every time we drove to a party. And Sumer had reminded me, according to the tab that he actually maintained on an app on his iPhone, that it was his turn to guzzle tonight.

'You can't waste alcohol. It's criminal!'

'Let's drink it neat.'

'And then puke it all out?'

'Let's call for it.'

'No one will deliver right now.'

'Then let's go out and get it. There's a twenty-four-hour petrol pump nearby, they'll have Coke and soda.'

Everyone loved the last idea.

'But who is going to drive down?'

Some pretended they didn't hear the question. Others simply looked down at their drinks, their shoes or the white marble floor—whatever got them out of the situation.

'I'll go.'

A valiant masculine voice was heard. Belonging to a man who is often known to exhibit charitable virtues under the influence of uncharitable liquids.

'Sumer, you're a rock star.' Liaka planted a kiss on his cheek and looked at me as she did it.

Those evil eyes.

Everyone hooted. And got back to their business. The music was turned on again.

'I'll come along.' I held Sumer's hand as he pulled out his keys from his pocket. Even if North Korea and South Korea's peace treaty depended on this, there was no chance in hell that I was going to stay back. Not with Liaka, alone.

'Tanie—'

'NO,' Liaka cut Sumer off. 'It's too late for her to go out. And you know how Delhi is.' She smiled like an angel and Sumer let go of my hand.

'You stay, Tan Tan.'

'Sumer, I—'

He pressed his finger on my lips.

Clearly not sober.

I didn't want to argue and create a scene. It would just mean a victory for Liaka.

'I'll take Konarak along.'

'Me, okay...yes,' said the same friend who was trying to flirt with me earlier.

Sumer then called out to another friend, who walked over. 'Ruhi...take care of her. She's...' he hiccupped, 'special,' he whispered in her ear and left with Konarak.

Ruhi and I walked over to a couch and sat down.

'You know, he keeps talking about you.'

'Yeah?'

'Yup. He's a good guy, Tanie.'

'I know.'

'Ruhi...' someone called out and she excused herself.

As I sat there alone, sipping my drink, Liaka sashayed up to me. With two minions in tow.

'So, Tanie, we finally get to talk. Sorry I couldn't attend to you properly in the last two hours... It's really brave of you to come to a party where you hardly know anyone.' Her voice was tight.

I felt the backs of my ears burn. And took a large sip of my drink.

Much better. Bring it on now, bitch.

'It's okay, Liaka. Sumer's been taking good care of me.'

I smiled. She frowned.

Liaka—1. Tanie—1.

'So how do you like Delhi? Must be crazy, right? I mean coming from something as small as Chandigarh...you must be all excited to be in a big city?'

Her minions smirked.

'Oh, it's been a highly entertaining experience. I mean, I got to meet you. Doesn't get better now, does it?'

The smirks died.

Liaka—2. Tanie—2.

'I'm sure you find it entertaining. You must have gotten bored of auditioning for *Roadies* and *Splitsvilla*. A lot of people from your city do that, right?'

'I wouldn't know, Liaka. I had an interesting life back home. Didn't really get the time to watch those shows.'

Liaka—3. Tanie—3.

'Obviously. How could I forget? You've had a pretty

interesting life. Stealing someone's boyfriend must be some serious amount of cheap thrills.'

The slap came impulsively. Everyone heard it. She began crying.

No. I'm kidding.

I put a smile on my face, a hand on her shoulder for support and got up. 'Liaka.' I lowered my eyes. 'Grow up. And while you're at it,' I froze my gaze just where it was needed,' 'grow some more of it as well. And oh, nice…flat. Not as huge as my house…but nonetheless. I'll go get myself a drink now.'

Liaka—3. Tanie—10.

I winked at her and walked off to the bar trolley, thanking God that I had finally filled out.

'I just told your ex she's flat. You might want to come back quickly. I'm in the mood for a catfight. And you'll be driving me back now. I'm going for the drinks,' I texted Sumer as I told a random guy to pour me a neat vodka with ice.

'Haha. NO. You've cock-blocked me enough. Coming in ten. And please don't drink,' he texted back. Immediately.

I smiled as I absent-mindedly reached out to pick up the glass. I was just about to take a sip, when…

'Oops.'

'What the fuck!'

'I'm so sorry. I didn't see you.' Liaka blinked apologetically.

The vodka had spilled down the front of my dress and trickled down to my midriff. I shot her a venomous look.

'The washroom's there. Second door on the left.' She smiled, pointing to a door.

Liaka—50. Tanie—10.

'Sure. No problem.'

'What the fuck!' she shrieked

'Oops. Sorry.' The glass I was holding had 'accidentally' slipped from my hand and broken, its pieces spraying all over her feet.

'The washroom is the second door to the left, right?'
Liaka—50. Tanie—100.
Burrrrnnn!

'Sumer, where the fuck are you?' I mumbled to myself as I tried to latch the washroom door. Unsuccessfully. I peeked out into the room again. It was empty. Hoping that no one would enter, I quickly dashed to the basin and opened the tap.

'FUCCCK!' I shut the tap as a volcanic stream of water suddenly erupted in the sink, spewing at me. Irritated, I looked around for the hand towels, only to find all of them already used up. Desperate, I picked up the toilet paper roll and had just started to clean myself, when...

'What the—'

'FUCK!'

An exhale from a strong jawline carved under an intentional three-day stubble. Built arms. Strong hands. One of them holding a bottle of beer. A tattoo peeking out from under his sleeve.

'I'm so sorry! I thought the washroom was empty.'

The deep voice. Enchanting.

'The latch isn't working,' I managed to utter.

He smirked. Crooked. Lighting up the resident mischief in his deep eyes. He walked over to me. I felt my knees give way. It couldn't be the alcohol.

'Do you mind if I get some...'

'Some?'

'Toilet paper as well?'

'What?'

'Yeah.' He pointed blatantly to his crotch. A large stain. 'Beer. They've gone crazy waiting for the mixers outside,' he said as he took the roll from my hand, infusing the air around me with the musk of the very familiar cologne he was wearing.

Blip. And my heartbeat went irregular. I closed my eyes to take a deeper whiff. He must have thought I was a retard. He laughed. I gathered myself.

'I haven't seen you at the party before? Have you been inside the washroom all this while?' he asked.

'I didn't know you were from the RSVP department here?' The tongue came back. And how. Phew! Some salvation there.

He raised his eyebrows. 'Interesting.' He leant against the sink and kept staring at me. 'Okay, this may sound like a pickup line, but you look familiar.'

'That's because you were racing with our car sometime back and you won.' The words left my mouth faster than they should have.

'He took a sip from his beer bottle. 'As they say, it's a small world. Kabir.' He held out his hand.

'Tanie,' I said, not shaking it.

You can't make them feel you're easy, even if you want to be sleazy. Men are hunters. The thrill is in the chase.

He retracted his hand. Took out what looked like a thinner version of a cigarette and put it in his mouth. 'Light?'

And he killed everything in that moment.

JOINTS. CHEMICALS. DRUGS. SMOKING. REPULSION.

Yes, I drank like a fish. And puked with capacity. Yes, I indulged. No, I did not want to sound like a hypocrite, but then again, there are certain things or habits you simply cannot stand, that you want to burn, castrate and expunge the very seed of from the face of this earth, no matter how much of a non-judgemental Mother Teresa you are. Drugs, for me, topped that list. They would for you too, if you, at fifteen, had lost an elder cousin, who was more than a sibling to you, to it.

'You know, there are better ways to kill yourself,' I said, walking out.

He held me by the hand and stopped me.

'Excuse me?'

He let go. 'Don't worry. I was just testing you.'

'Sorry?'

'You know. You're a pretty girl. And by the sound of it, an intelligent one. I was just checking how sorted you are.' He flicked the joint into the pot. And scored. Big time brownie points.

'Can I make a call from your mobile?'

He must have thought that I was giving him my number. He handed it to me.

'Hello, Justdial? Yeah…hi, could you give me the number of a few psychologists who treat arrogant, bratty young guys?'

Even he hadn't seen this coming.

I cut the call. 'They've messaged you the numbers. Good luck with that.'

'You're amazing. Let's start over.'

'Why do you think I care?'

'Coz you do. You would have walked off way earlier if you didn't.'

He had me floored. I smiled.

'Tanie.'

'Kabir. So Tanie, you're not a friend of Liaka's, for sure.'

Did he see what I did to her outside?

'What makes you say that?'

'When it comes to friendship, there's a calibre that clicks. You're way above the host.'

A blush crept up on my cheeks. I quickly shrugged it off.

'And you're at this party because you hate her?' I retorted.

'I'm technically here coz we share a small amount of genetics…we're cousins.'

'Oops.'

'Don't worry. I like her as much as I think you do.'

'Haha. Well...'

'So who are you here with?'

'I'm with—'

'Tanie!' Sumer stumbled in, panting. 'Answer your goddamn phone! I've been looking for you all over...' He looked at Kabir.

The eye-lock. The race. The men. The ego. Kabir's smirk. Sumer's nostrils. Both flared.

'Let's go.' He grabbed my hand.

I shot an apologetic look at Kabir, who stood there, unaffected.

Like a man. Not a boy.

Sumer walked out and I trudged along. We went back to the living room. The same music. The same people. Liaka. With changed shoes and a scowl. The same level of chaos.

'What were you doing inside with him?' Sumer asked me as he poured himself another drink.

Kabir had come out as well and was secretly glancing at me as he stood at a distance with a girl, not paying attention to what she was saying.

'Huh?' Sumer caught me red-handed.

'Why don't you just go and stand with him?'

'I told you, Sumer, YOUR Liaka dropped the drink on me. And I just went to clean it. And he is HER cousin. Don't you know him?'

'Maybe...yeah...I think I've seen him before. But fuck that...fuck him.'

'You're just jealous coz you lost the race to him.' I laughed.

'Me?' he scoffed. 'Yeah, right!'

Someone played Honey Singh and Sumer grabbed my wrist. 'Enough with the talking.'

I kept stealing glances at Kabir as Sumer and I danced, while Liaka hovered around, accidentally falling into Sumer's arms time and again. Kabir kept standing in a corner, doing his own thing. There was so much I wanted to do. With him. To him. And he didn't even come up to me and try to strike up a conversation! Though he continued to eye me.

And then, just when I had given up all hope, Coldplay whipped up some mush with soft music on the playlist and he walked up to me. Sumer had his arm around my waist.

Kabir held out his hand. Firmly.

I looked at Sumer. Longingly.

He rolled his eyes. In forced approval.

I smiled.

Kabir pulled me towards him. With intention.

Liaka, seizing the opportunity, crept up to Sumer and started to rub her nose against his. He was so drunk now, he could do a giraffe. I knew he would soon disappear into a room. And come back stained. It happened, soon enough.

Kabir and I, in the meantime, got ourselves drinks and went out to the terrace. With enough alcohol in my system by now to fearlessly proclaim, I talked while he listened politely, punctuating my college, Sumer and Chandigarh rants with sincere smiles.

He briefly filled me in on his life. He was twenty-two. Born and brought up in Delhi. Just out of college. Lived in Vasant Kunj. And was working with his dad at his construction firm. He remembered Sumer as Liaka's boyfriend from two years ago.

'I've got to go. It was great sharing that toilet paper, a dance and this drink with you, ma'am.' Kabir chugged the remains of his drink.

'Oh...okay.' I tried hard to hide my displeasure. Sumer was still in the room with Liaka.

'Need to take my kid sister out in the morning to Hamleys. Or she will butcher me.' He smiled.

'Cool.'

Never Kiss Your Best Friend 95

He winked and turned to leave.

No number. No WhatsApp. No goddamn BBM pin, even.

He turned around again. Held my hand and kissed it without permission. The old-school way. And left.

It was only after he left that I realized he had thrust a small chit of paper into my hand.

It read, '*You know what the good thing is about having a bad cousin? Nothing. But you're beautiful. And it was great meeting you.*'

You know those moments when you want to shout out loud because you're extremely happy and sad at the same time? Yes, I went through one of them right then.

It was the start of something new.

Just that I did not have his number to start it. Neither did he have mine.

Nuclear bombs. Terrorism. Poverty. HIV/AIDS. Cancer. Gaddafi. Rakhi Sawant. Sexy boys who charm you at parties and then leave without giving you their number.

And HANGOVERS.

If only they did not exist.

I got up with an apocalyptic feeling the next afternoon and started the patented teenage morning routine of checking my phone first.

Three missed calls from Mom. Manageable.

Ten WhatsApp messages from friends at college and random group chats. Ignorable.

Nothing from Kabir. WHY?

Nothing from Sumer. HIM!

Last night after Kabir had left, I had chilled with Ruhi till Sumer came out, after an hour, tired and drunk beyond repair, with a dented and painted neck. I had whined to him about the edible but painfully mysterious Kabir while he had called for a cab, leaving his car at Liaka's. He had passed out in the cab as soon as we set off for my PG and only woke up when I got off, telling me dreamily that he was going back home. Or perhaps not!

I called Sumer groggily as I got a bottle of water from the portable fridge in my room. He didn't answer. I was his best friend. I had a right to know everything he did. At whatever hour of the night. Or day. With whomsoever. And in whatever position.

The call went unanswered again.

Regretting every drop of alcohol that I had drunk last night—until I drank again, that is—I showered, ate, started downloading another season of *Game of Thrones* using my landlady's Wi-Fi and then finally logged onto Facebook to check the pictures, if there were any, from last night. And yes, if Kabir was tagged in them. And had also checked them and messaged me or sent a friend request.

Nothing. No pictures. No message. No friend request.

Of all the words uttered in tongue and ink, 'what if' bleed the most.

What if I had stopped acting cool and asked for his number? What if I hadn't let him go and had kissed those perfectly moulded lips? What if?

An untimely, unannounced feeling of sadness crept through my veins and was making its way to my heart when my phone rang. Thinking it would be Sumer, I answered. 'Done emptying your pea-sized dick on her tits? That hot cunt hasn't called or messaged yet.'

I heard a deep manly cough of amusement from the other end. 'I didn't particularly know you liked hot cunts. Or sounded so classy, despite those utterances.'

I stiffened. That voice. I quickly checked the mobile screen. It said 'Private Number'. *Fancy.*

But fuck!

'Hot cunt here wants to ask you out tonight. Social? Hauz Khas Village? 8 p.m.? I'll pick you up?'

'Ummm...'

'Was that too forward?'

That apology soaked in honey. 'No! No! Okay! Cool...you know where I live?' I grinned like a toddler who had been visited by Santa.

'If I could find your number, I sure do know where you live. 8 p.m.'

'That's creepy.' Inherent sarcasm often finds a leak. Like a beer-filled belly. And my tongue.

He smiled. 'It sure is. But I couldn't help myself. You were worth the chase.' He cut the call.

It sure was creepy, but hot creepy. Like voyeurism. Or exhibitionism. Okay, maybe not that, but hot for sure. I somersaulted on my bed. Excited beyond fuck. I called Sumer immediately. And didn't stop till he answered.

'Tanie. If...*aahh*...if I'm...oh...that feels good... If I'm not answering your calls, there must be a...*oohhhh*...reason,' he moaned.

'Where are you?' I asked, already fearing the answer.

Sumer didn't reply. Instead, I heard a female voice in the background. 'Is this much pressure okay?'

Confirmed.

'Yuck, you're still at her house? How much sex will you have?'

'I'm at the SPA, Tanie.'

'Spa?'

'Yes. I was so hungover and tired, I needed a massage. It was a long night.'

'That's so gay.'

'Ask Liaka about that.' Then he whispered into the phone, 'It's time for a happy ending now. I'll talk to you later.'

I puked internally. 'Sumer, wait—'

The call was cut.

Angrily I called him back. He didn't answer. I sent him an array of WhatsApp messages with the most inventive abuses that my mind could come up with. He didn't bother responding to them either. With no other choice left, I did that-which-must-not-be-done.

I was applying one of those consumerism-fed, instant-glow face packs that actresses with not so much as a trace of a wrinkle on their flawless skins advertise on television when Sumer called back.

'I'm so sorry, Tanie! Which friend of yours hit the kid? Who are you with? You weren't driving, na? Which hospital are you in? I'll just be there!'

He sounded frantic. I felt guilty. Momentarily. And then a sadistic laugh from the greyer part of my soul killed it.

'You're such a slut!' he howled as he honked.

Coincidentally, he was driving.

'How was the happy ending?'

'Very funny.'

'Anyhow listen, there genuinely is an emergency,' I said gravely, checking if the face pack had dried. It hadn't.

'I'm driving, I'll call you once I get—'

'NO.' I didn't let him cut the call this time. 'Kabir asked me out tonight. Social. HKV,' I blurted impatiently.

'Who's Kabir?'

'Kabir!' My nostrils flared. 'Like you don't remember. Stop acting cool. He got my number from I don't know where but he's asked me out tonight…'

'Getting your number from "somewhere". That's creepy.'

'It's hot.'

He laughed.

I ignored him. And spoke cutely. For fuck's sake, I couldn't be mean to him right now.

'So...Sumeru...my baby doll...'

'Bark.' He was curt.

'Summu...I'm going to tell Mom that I'm going out with you for dinner and drinks. If she calls, please say I'm with you. I'll tell her I'll be back by no later than twelve.'

'No,' he replied flatly.

'Why?' My heart sank.

'Because I don't like that guy's vibe, Tanie. He looks smooth. And you only told me he's twenty-two. The last time you dated an older guy...' He left the sentence hanging.

'Since when did you get vibes from guys, Sumer? First the spa and then this... Are you sure you don't want to play for the other side?' I tried to diffuse the situation with humour, not wanting to think about the past.

'It's not a joke. It's like how you girls have a bitch-o-meter. We have a play-o-meter.'

'Sumer, what's your problem?' I was beginning to lose patience.

'That you get your heart broken and then come to me to get it nursed. So I'm warning you beforehand,' he said cockily.

'I can't believe you. I'm telling you, he's a good guy. I know him.'

'He isn't. Trust me, he's not worth the deal.'

'Oh yeah, then who is? You? Who kissed me and fell in love with me only to fuck around as soon as I said no? Stop being jealous!'

A sword stabs. A bomb blasts. A knife pierces. A fire burns. And when all of these fail, there are words.

He spoke after what seemed to be an eternity. 'Stop with the melodrama. I'll take care of Aunty if she calls.'

'I love you.' I kissed into the phone.

'Save it for tonight. Also, don't mix your drinks. Or go for more than two LIITs. And no Scotch. That's our thing. And...try not to get raped. And if you do, don't call me, I've got a date.'

'A date! How come I don't know about this?' I asked as a sudden wave of possessiveness struck me.

'If only you would let me speak. I'm going out with Liaka.'

'But you've already done her.'

'You're crass.'

I laughed out loud. 'I'm crass?'

'I think I like her. Let's see.'

'So where are you going?'

'I don't know. She says it's a surprise.'

My face pack had dried to the point where flexing my jaw to speak hurt. 'Cool,' I muttered, getting up to wash it off.

'Umm...Tan Tan...there's something...' He didn't need to finish the sentence.

'What did you do now?' I demanded.

'I have a confession to make. I think I came on Liaka's Armani cushion covers. She doesn't know.'

I laughed out loud. Like really loud. 'I'll message you when I'm getting ready, help me decide what to wear.'

'Only if I see you in your bra.'

'You wish.'

'Have a good time, Tan Tan.'

'I will. And thanks, I love you.'

'If you do, you'll send me a picture of you in your bra.'

'I'll think about it.'

He smiled. She smiled. Problem solved.

So you're a rich kid. And you completely hate that. And everything mainstream and commercial. Like malls. And anything musical that flows in regular beats. So what do you do then? You scoff at the Gucci moccasin-wearing junta, those with their turned-up Burberry collars, you wear your Aldo slippers and your Rohit Gandhi linen shirt, roll a joint—nothing less than Manali maal—carry a jhola with a MacBook Air in it while you chuck daal roti and butter chicken for falafel and hummus and come celebrate your 'brave' 'uncorrupted' existence at HKV.

What's HKV, bro?

You don't know HKV? That painfully put together bohemian (oxymoron, anyone?) market in South Delhi with 'shady', terraced restaurants and 'desi' cafés that serve decaf coffee for nothing less than a grand and designer stores that sell khadi at a price that would leave Gandhi naked if he were to come back to life?

C'mon, let's not bitch about the place. After all it's the mecca for hipsters.

And have you been to Hauz Khas Social?

Arre, this place with the completely chilled-out scene, with crazy food, crazier drinks frequented by crazy amounts of crazily good-looking and well-turned-out people who are crazy enough to sing along to songs they don't have a crazy idea about.

We reached Social. And it being a Saturday night, there was a decent-sized crowd waiting to get in.

If Sumer had been there, he would have thrown a drama queen tantrum about how hot it was and said, 'Let's just fuck this shit and go somewhere else.'

'Now what?' I wondered if Kabir would annoy me equally.

Kabir smiled to dispel my apprehensions. 'We make our way through.'

He took my hand, guided me through the crowd and smiled

at the manager taking down names at the door. And the manager opened the door for us. I got a few envious looks from the girls around me. Maybe because I did look hot in the sleeveless pink-and-blue Zara dress I had worn at Sumer's insistence. Maybe because I got to get in before my body mist and make-up could give way and I didn't smell like a tuna sandwich from Subway. Maybe because my accessory was hotter than the ones they were holding onto. And no, I'm not referring to the bags they were carrying.

Every girl deserves to feel like a queen. And today, I was with royalty.

Kabir said 'hi' and shot smiles at quite a few people as we made our way to our table. Yes, he was connected.

Or maybe he just brought you to a place where he knows everyone, Tanie, I imagined Sumer saying while scratching his balls shamelessly in front of me as I told him about this night.

I had to stop thinking about that ass. And comparing them.

'Tanie?'

I snapped back to the present and smiled as Kabir pulled out the chair for me.

Wasn't this getting too much now? This after he picked me up on time, looking bloody hot in a white linen shirt—teasingly unbuttoned enough for me to secretly glance at his sculpted chest—with blue denims and smart loafers. And then Kabir had opened every door for me. And let me play music from my phone in the car. Sumer would have a cardiac arrest laughing if I told him how courteous Kabir was. For he wasn't the type who would open doors, or carry handkerchiefs, or leave the last piece of pizza for you, even out of courtesy. And this change was welcome, to say the least. I laughed. Another subconscious comparison.

Kabir noticed.

The waiter came over and we ordered starters. I didn't want

to look like a hog, even though I hadn't eaten anything since his call that afternoon, so I killed the urge in my stomach and politely asked for a chicken Caesar salad and some red wine.

'C'mon now, we're not eating leaves here or drinking stale wine. French fries, chicken wings. And get us two LIITs.'

A hungry, lusty-for-foodgasm grin surfaced on my lips.

The waiter came back with the LIITs and the food. Our glasses clinked. And the plate of French fries was polished off in no time.

'The last time you laughed, before we ordered, you were thinking about someone else,' he said as I was in the middle of struggling with a chicken wing, trying to slice it without ripping it apart. Like how Sumer and I always went for the kill.

'Huh?'

'I said, the last time you laughed, before we ordered, you were thinking about someone else.'

'I…I…fuck that, you tell me, how did you guess?' I gave up on the chicken wing.

'At one point of time, my life was all about reading minds and negotiating with speed.'

I looked lost. And defeated as the chicken wing stared back at me, victorious.

He explained. 'I was training to become an F1 racer, Tanie. And contrary to what people think, it's more of a mind game than just accelerating the pedal.'

'So why did you stop?'

He chugged his LIIT pensively.

Confused, I took a few delicate sips in silence. 'It's okay if you don't want to talk…aaaahhh,' I ended abruptly.

He had caught me unawares as he brushed his foot against my bare leg.

'This foot…the one that just touched you…it touched the accelerator very hard one day on the Buddh Circuit. I was twenty back then... It was a regular day and I was doing my routine laps and then one incorrectly negotiated turn changed it all. Six months in bed. And a warning not to strain my ankle, which now had an artificial ball in it. It was a bad accident and I took it in a worse manner.'

He took out a joint from his wallet.

'I was in rehab for six months. But I've been clean ever since.'

I looked at him, too shocked to process all that he had suddenly thrown at me.

'Then why do you carry a joint with you?' I asked very slowly.

'I keep one with me all the time, to remind me of who I was, what I became.' He didn't blink as he stared at me. 'And who I can become, if I let go of it,' he said, crushing the joint.

'Yesterday, the car race...it...it just took me back to those days. And when I saw you, it's funny and cheesy and you may want to run away from this table on hearing this, but that moment...behind the wheel, the joint in my pocket and you in my rearview...it felt different...a nice different...a different that made me want to live life with that "different", differently.'

I squeezed his hand. And he linked his fingers with mine. In this story of tears and a stained heart, there hadn't been a moment so complete. Like nothing or no one mattered.

'Tan Tan, what a pleasantttt surpriiiise.'

NO. This drunken rant. This voice. THIS MAN. SUMER!

'Hi guys.' A visibly gone and surprisingly pleasant Liaka, in hot pants and a top, shot Kabir and ME a smile!

Sumer's eyes were bloodshot. And had a certain vacant look to them that I hadn't seen before. Like he had mixed and guzzled all the alcohol in the bar. And then drained bottles of cough syrup to add to the effect.

'What are you doing here, Sumer?' I tried my best to make the question sound pleasant.

It clearly did not work.

'Liaka brought me here. I swear.' He raised his hands to prove he hadn't crossed any fingers.

The backs of my ears burned on seeing Kabir getting amused by all of this. My best friend, who first acted like a jerk, was now embarrassing me. Perfect, just perfect.

'So, Tanie, is he the new catch?' Liaka slurred with a smile, scooping up some French fries from the plate. Without permission. Of course.

'Oh! Even I'm so hungry!' Sumer followed suit.

I had full intention to stab Sumer with the butter knife kept on the table. Luckily, Kabir's phone rang just then and he excused himself. Liaka slumped unceremoniously on the chair Kabir had occupied as soon as he left. That ticked me off.

'What the fuck is happening here?' I demanded, looking at Sumer.

His lips lifted into a mischievous smile as he raised his index finger, turned around and walked over to the washroom. He almost banged into a waiter as he made his way through.

Liaka continued to smile, eyeing all the food.

'What the fuck is your problem, Liaka?' I killed the urge to strangle her. Somehow. She continued to smile. Like a drunk bitch.

'Enough!' Seething with anger, I got up and walked to the washroom.

Sumer had taken it too far this time. And it genuinely wasn't funny. I knocked violently on the door of the men's toilet. A girl came out of the women's toilet.

'Take it easy, woman.' She winked.

I just looked down at my feet.

This couldn't get more embarrassing.

I knocked again. He didn't reply.

'Sumer! Come out, you m***fucker! I swear, if you don't

open the door, I'll call security and get you kicked out and I MEAN IT,' I hissed, my lips stuck to the door.

I heard my own panting and the lock click open. I went in and locked the door immediately. He was sitting on the pot with his head down. The sink was overflowing with water. And toilet paper swam in it.

Acting the part, very clever.

'Stop it. It's not funny anymore!' I went and shook him by his shoulders.

He pretended to stir and looked up at me, with lost eyes, like I had woken him up from slumber.

Wiping a river of sweat from his forehead, he smiled goofily as he sang my name.

'Tanieee.'

'I swear I'll slap you if you don't stop now. I've been drinking with you for two goddamn years, I know you never get so drunk. I know you're doing all of this just because you think he isn't a good guy!'

'I'm not drunk, Tanie...I'm flying.'

Another irritating smirk.

'Why are you doing this? Kabir is actually a nice guy... Stop judging people and making choices for me. And I can't believe you've teamed up with Liaka... Seriously?'

Someone knocked on the door.

'We're busy,' I shouted, angrily wiping away a tear.

'Yes, shut up, we're busy in here,' Sumer added, loudly.

'Umm, Tanie, is everything okay?'

It was Kabir.

Petrified, I quickly cleared my throat. 'K...Kabir...Sumer's not well. I'll be out in a minute.'

'You sure?'

I sensed the disappointment in his voice through the door. Finding your date locked in the men's toilet with her drunk best friend can do that to you.

I swallowed the heavy lump in my throat. Wiping the tears that continued to flow, I said sullenly, 'Thanks, Sumer. Thanks for fucking it up for me. I hope you stay happy in your life. Because from this moment on, this friendship is over.'

I didn't wait for a response. I walked out of the washroom and met Kabir.

'Are you all right?'

'Ummm…Kabir…can we leave?'

'Shouldn't we wait for your friend? Liaka is also waiting at the table. And she looks pretty wasted,' he said, concerned.

If only Sumer could see all of this.

'No. It's okay. Sumer's fine. He can take care of her.' I smiled half-heartedly. 'Let's go?'

'Anything for you, ma'am,' he said without asking any more questions.

I looked away. The tears were threatening to make their existence felt again. He paid the tab. We left. Got to the car. And drove back in silence. A boulder of guilt weighed me down, preventing me from saying anything to him.

We were crossing India Gate when Kabir suddenly stopped the car.

'Ice cream.'

'No.'

He had already gotten out of the car. And opened the passenger door for me. He held out his hand. 'I'm not asking.'

I got out. It was 11.30 p.m. on a Saturday night. The India Gate gardens were filled with families in the forefront and couples behind the bushes. We got ice creams from an Amul ice-cream cart. Two orange popsicles. We started to walk back to the car.

'You know, Tanie, as a kid, whenever I got angry with Mom and Dad, they would bring me here for ice cream.' He tore the wrapper off for me. I took a reluctant bite, still not feeling up to it.

'They'd say that the best way to pacify anger is to melt it down with something so sweet that you forget what anger tastes like... I believed in what they said.'

We reached the car and stood leaning against the bonnet.

'They got divorced when I was ten,' he spoke softly as we stood, slurping on our popsicles. 'And for a really long time, I was angry with them for it. The people who had taught me how to deal with anger couldn't handle their own anger and solve their own problems... I spent a couple of years in denial. But then one day, I came here, to India Gate and ate a popsicle alone and realized that sometimes, you've just got to love the choices you've made. It's worth the effort.

'Sumer's a nice guy, Tanie. He was just concerned. Don't worry. I had a great time. And I really want to take this forward.'

He took a bite from his popsicle and a trickle of ice ran down his chin. Fully aware of who I was, what I was doing and where I was, I inched forward and traced my tongue from his chin to his lips, only to meet his tongue. We kissed. Softly. At India Gate. And in that moment, I knew I had found love. And I wasn't going to let go of it. Even if my best friend didn't approve.

Ever.

'I haven't tasted love, but I think it tastes like orange', I typed in my Facebook status bar and then, in a rational blink of the eye, deleted it, minutes after Kabir dropped me home.

Finally it felt right, after two long years.

It's a generational thing. You update it first and feel it later.

I called up Megha. Then Stuti. Even Amrita and Raunak from college. And told them everything about Kabir. And the night. Keeping Sumer's presence and actions to a bare minimum.

Megha and Stuti, despite the different latitudes, time zones and accents (yes, Megha was already AMARICAN) shrieked happily in the same manner in the beginning, only to finish the conservation with a buzz kill.

'So, is Sumer cool with this?'

Sumer...

The mature part of me wanted to forgive him and call him right away and tell him how edible Kabir's lips were. But as the night changed colours, the shades of maturity dwindled into the solid wash of egotism.

I decided to wait for him to call or message. Which he did, three painfully long days later. And killed his only shot at the salvation of our friendship.

Three days later.

WhatsApp chat window

Tanie online	
Sumer typing...	
Tanie online	1:53 p.m.
Sumer last seen at 1:56 p.m.	
Tanie online	3:47 p.m.
Sumer typing...	
Tanie Status If you have the BALLS to fuck it up, have the BALLS to apologize for it. And not just TYPE and not send the message.	4:56 p.m.

Sumer Status	4:59 p.m.
Apology for a mistake, the finger for an accusation.	
Tanie Status	5:03 p.m.
EGO. Shove it up your ass with all the fingers you want to raise.	
Sumer Status	5:06 p.m.
They shout in your ears that they want a good boy. Then they shout at you when you tell them they've chosen a bad boy. Sincerely—a best friend tired of handing out tissues.	
Tanie Status	5:09 p.m.
Long statuses. Sincerely—defining a guilt trip.	
Sumer Status	5:13 p.m.
The guilty start a status war. The pure simply type.	
Tanie Status	5:17 p.m.
Exactly. If only you finished typing the message!	
Sumer: last seen at 5:19 p.m.	

'Yes, I won!' I smiled into my phone as Amrita, my friend from college, handed me the plate of chicken tandoori dim sums.

We were chilling at QDs. Legend has it, if you're studying in DU and don't have the chicken tandoori dim sums there, your forehead shall always carry an inscription that starts with a 'c' and ends with an 'a'.

'What did you win?' Amrita asked casually as she licked the chilly sauce off her fingertips.

She had seen me frantically pull out my cell during class, then later under the 'virgin tree' as we sipped chai, then as we shopped at K-Nags or Kamla Nagar market (for the uninitiated), but she obviously didn't know that I wasn't merely texting, I was fighting a crusade and I had won.

But my victory was short-lived.

'Sumer and you fought. And no, it isn't a question,' Stuti announced as soon as I answered her call, the very next second.

'Yes. And no,' I said defensively.

'He's on the other line. Suck it up and sort it out. And no, he hasn't told me anything, so I'm not on his side already. I've been having a good laugh over his and your WhatsApp statuses, but enough now.'

Before I could say anything, she added him to the call.

'I'm out with Mom for some stupid family-function shopping...don't cut the call, you two. I'm going on mute but I'll check,' she instructed us like a schoolteacher.

'I'm mature enough to have a conversation...unlike other people, Stuti,' Sumer yapped.

'Stuti, since when did mature people spend their evenings drunk out of their minds, sitting on a bathroom pot in a lounge on Saturday night? All of it to intentionally fuck their friend's shot at...' I paused to find the correct word, 'love.'

'Stuti, because they know that the guy their friend is falling in "love" with is shady.'

'Stuti, have you been watching *Sherlock* too? Clearly a lot of people can't handle it.'

'So have you two sorted it out?' Stuti suddenly said.

As it turned out, she had already put us on mute and we hadn't realized it. We both killed the urge to laugh. This was serious.

'Ummm—' Sumer tried to think of a comeback.

I took a deep breath. I was tired of this. A great future was at the doorstep of my life and I didn't want to step into it leaving behind a greater past. 'Sumer...can we talk?' I addressed him directly.

'Yes Mom, take the pink sari...no, Mom, not the bright pink one...it's hurting my eyes...the sober pink...no, not that, it's hardly pink...take something in between...' Stuti whined, interjecting at an important moment.

'Baby pink, maybe?' Sumer murmured.

'Wow, Sumer, that's pretty macho, you know a lot about pink. Okay, yes Mom...baby pink...right...wait, I'll help you...I'll talk to you two in a bit...continue.' She put us on mute again.

I laughed. He was too cute to fight with anymore. 'My pink Dhillon, why are we doing this?'

'Because I care for you, Tanie.'

'He's a nice guy. I'm sure of that. And I'll be careful, if he isn't. Trust me when I say this...this one is really special.'

'Already? In two meetings and four days?'

'We met yesterday too.'

'Okay then...three meetings and four days.'

Amrita signalled to me. She was getting late. It was evening. And this was Delhi. I began to walk back to her Activa.

'Sumer, I have to go now. But we're cool, right?' I said, sitting pillion.

'We're always cool, Tanie, but that guy Kabir isn't. So, I

didn't message you in the last three days, coz I...I...I found out stuff about him.' He took a dramatic pause. 'Meet me in the evening...I'll drive down to wherever you say.'

Amrita turned on the ignition, but I got off, scared, and begged her to wait for two more minutes. She reluctantly complied, knowing I meant ten.

'What do you mean?' I asked sombrely as I walked away from the Activa.

Sumer had said the same words when he had busted Rehaan... Meet me Tanie, I'll tell you everything.

'Meet me...I'll tell you everything,' he repeated the omen.

'Just tell me now!' I hissed into the phone.

'He's got a reputation, Tanie. I tried asking Liaka and she didn't have much to say, just that he was in rehab for six months.'

'Ahhh. Thank God.' I laughed out loud.

'Are you okay? I told you we should meet and discuss this,' Sumer asked, thinking I hadn't taken the news well and was going crazy in the middle of a busy market.

'I know all about it, Sumer. He's told me everything. I know I detest, no, actually loathe people who do drugs and when he told me about the rehab bit...I wanted to just walk away...but he had a reason...his eyes...they were honest...so it's okay...'

'Tanie?'

I started to walk back to the Activa. 'Hmmm?'

'Would you judge me if I told you something?'

'I always judge you, Dhillon.'

'That night at Social, I wasn't—'

Amrita honked and I cut Sumer off. 'I know you weren't so drunk. Good job with the acting though, even that bitch is a good actor.'

'What?' He cleared his throat. 'Yeah...yeah. Liaka's a good actor.'

I sat on the Activa. Amrita brought it to life, shooting me a deadly look, of course.

'Okay now, I'll call you once I'm home. Amrita has plans to kill me. Goodbye Stuti, if you've been hearing all of this, silently.'

I was about to cut the call when Sumer spoke again. 'Don't date him.'

I lost my patience. 'WHAT THE FUCK, SUMER!'

A biker parallel to us craned his neck. I was that loud, even in the moving traffic. Amrita zipped her Activa faster. Girls. Evening. Delhi. Enough said.

'Don't ask me questions, just don't date him.'

'Sumer.' I thrust the phone closer to my mouth, 'If you're a friend, you will not say this again. Otherwise, it's purely your call, I will be there for you, even if you don't want to be there for me. Bye.'

I cut the call.

And he did not call back.

Some declare love happens over a lifetime, while others say it takes a casual blink of an eye.

I think somewhere between those extremes, I found my footing. And stuck to it. I was in love.

Kabir and I started to date. With a vengeance, doing what most couples do. Talking to each other twenty-four hours a day. Obsessively spamming each other's Facebook accounts. Retweeting each other's tweets. Inundating each other's Instagram accounts with our selfies. Sharing our passwords and ATM pins. Addressing each other with those diabetic mushy names. Saying 'I love you' to each other before saying 'Hi'. Sitting on the same side of the table to eat so that we felt secure.

And going on dates, hand in hand, wearing colour-coordinated clothes and underwear.

Not really.

We would laugh together at all the couples who did all of that. Yes, we met a lot. During the day and night. But we never crossed the line of our individual comfort. We would go out drinking. Watch action movies. Go clubbing with his or my friends. Check out hot guys and slutty girls for each other. And when we got bored of doing all of that we would make out like bunnies in all the wrong places—at the movies, in the car, in his room while his younger sister sat outside watching *Shin Chan*, just to keep the thrill intact.

Even though we hadn't yet said it to each other, we felt it. That this wasn't just 'another' relationship. And those three words wouldn't come out in a drunken rush anytime soon but whenever they did, they would be an emotional whisper.

He was everything I wanted. Alcoholic but not an addict. Arousing but not a horny guy with a perennial hand in his pants who pushed me to have sex with him until I was ready. Well-built but not a gym trainer. Caring but not intrusive. Protective but not obsessive.

And I also made sure that I gave him all the space, the trust and the reasons not to regret the night we had met inside a washroom.

October rolled over to November, which gave way to December. I visited home. Came back richer. Emotionally and financially. Friendships in college got deeper. I started to have 'legitimate' nightouts. I joined the editorial board of the college newspaper. Made even more friends there. The chilling scene became intense after that. Maggi at Uncle Tom's. Pizza at PAM centre. Sleepovers at Amrita's. Ladies' nights with Sonya. Study sessions for the semester exams at Saraansh's house, where we decided to make Maggi in rum instead of water and puked our guts out the next morning, before the exam.

The last three months had given me so many new memories. Of love. And friendship.

It's not like Sumer and I cut off from each other. But we distanced ourselves. Not blatantly, with a public spat and hurled abuses but silently, with unsaid words and a moist heart. And it hurt. But time bandaged the wound, even if it couldn't heal it completely. Like an old photograph that loses its clarity but never loses the outline of the image it holds, our friendship survived but somehow ceased to thrive.

It obviously began with Kabir. Then Sumer started officially dating Liaka and didn't bother telling me. I came to know about it through Facebook. It hurt me, not because he was dating a bitch or that he didn't feel the need to tell me himself, but because he started dating her two days after we had argued over the phone about Kabir, in September. I let go of it and called to congratulate him. And he acted all cool and icy about it. That was the final incident which triggered the cycle. Movie plans got cancelled. Beer drinking sessions postponed. WhatsApp messages were answered the next day. Calls were ignored. Our meetings became rare, shorter and curt. Unapologetic laughter turned to forced smiles. Comfortable silence into obligatory dialogues.

Kabir never had a problem with him. I don't know about Liaka, though. Yet, things changed. He chose his life. I chose mine. And from being a 'need' we became a 'choice' for each other. But then we met again. In December.

And almost died.

'Mom…I'm so sorry…I love you. And I miss you.'

It was her birthday. I had been out clubbing with Kabir the previous night and had forgotten to wish Mom at midnight. Needless to say, I was feeling terrible about it.

'It's okay, Tanie. So what if you didn't wish me last night? You must have gotten tired studying.'

Mothers, they know when you're lying and they make sure you know that too, even without saying it. 'I miss you too, Tanie. And I know you love me.' Mom could no longer control her tears.

Dad snatched the phone from her, walked out of the room and whispered into the phone, 'Tanie.'

'Why are you whispering, Dad?'

'Your mom is missing you.'

'I know. And she told me you haven't gifted her anything yet. If I get a husband like this…' Suddenly Kabir's face flashed in front of my eyes and I blinked it away, feeling eerie. '…I'll divorce him.'

Dad laughed awkwardly. 'Her cupboard is overflowing with everything, beta.'

'Dad, I'm going to tell you this and you better understand.' I uttered like a pious sermon, 'A woman's cupboard always has enough space for a pair of classic Jimmy Choos.'

He laughed and I heard a door close in the background. He had come to the washroom, for his voice echoed. 'Your mother has trained you well. Okay, now listen, I wasn't supposed to tell you this for another two hours…but I've decided to do something special for her today evening…something she or even you would never expect from me.'

Imagination. It's a disturbing art your mind possesses. I shooed away the collage of images that came to my mind as I heard the excitement in Dad's mid-life-crisis-induced voice. Candles. Handcuffs. Feathers. A private strip show. Role play. And them. My parents.

DISGUSTING.

Are you making a sibling for me? Now, at forty-eight?

'I am baking her a cake.'

'This is your special plan?' I retorted, disappointed and relieved at the same time.

'No, beta, that's just part of the plan. I've called all her friends, Sumer's mom helped me. Even your mom's...' this he said with disgust, like a true husband, 'dirty relatives are coming...and I've called the caterers...her favourite cuisine... Aarti will take her out in the evening. And she'll come back to a house full of roses and people she loves.' He got lost in his vision.

I knew he had to be kidding about this. Dad wouldn't put down the toilet seat if he had his way. This much effort would have caused him paralysis.

'Okay. Who are you and what have you done to my father?'

Dad laughed again. 'Your mother deserves it. She's done so much for me, for you. Looking after my friends every time they come over, ignoring hers, making my life her life, meeting me with a smile the next morning even if I shouted at her the night before. It's time I paid back.'

Wow! Either Dad had gotten drunk with his early morning golf buddies or he had had a serious fall last night.

'Okay. I'm seriously scared now, Dad. What's up?'

'I'm serious, beta. The party is on tonight.'

'C'mon, Dad. If this is a joke, it's really not funny. Just go and get Mom a gift, instead of annoying me.' I was getting irritated now.

Daddies and their ways of getting back at their teenage daughters who don't call them often from college.

'Beta, I'm serious. And I know you don't expect me to do something like this, but it's all for a reason. And you'll know this evening.'

This wasn't the man who loved my mother, yet irritated her with his typically male qualities. This wasn't the man who threw tantrums at dinner. Who would wake my mother up at

2 a.m. to get him a glass of cold milk. Who forgot to pick up her clothes from the dry-cleaner before my cousin's wedding. Who would make sure the entire house got up every morning before he left for his daily game of golf.

This man was behaving unlike his ball-scratching fraternity. This was the kind of husband they talked about in the movies.

Then realization hit me. 'And you're telling me now?' I looked at my watch. 'At 10 a.m.? How am I supposed to get home by the evening? The evening Shatabdi train to Chandigarh leaves at six! And I'll only be there by ten…OHMYGOD…let me check the flights!' I dashed to the laptop.

'Tanie!' my father shouted to calm me down. 'I didn't tell you earlier because even you know how good you are at keeping secrets. Everything is taken care of. Sumer is coming to pick you up at twelve. He's driving you down to Chandigarh.'

'What? Who?'

'Sumer, beta.'

Okay, this morning was getting too much to handle. I needed a drink. Or a fan and a rope.

'Yes, I planned it all out with Aarti. I've been assured he's a safe driver and has a licence. He'll be there at twelve. Be ready.'

'But, I…' I stopped. Obviously, our parents had no idea about what had happened in the last three months.

I had no choice but to agree. My mother's happiness and father's excitement were paramount. I couldn't be so selfish.

'Okay, Dad. Bye. I need to get ready.'

'See you in the evening, beta.'

I cut the call and instantly called Kabir to tell him everything. Especially stressing that Sumer was driving me down.

'Go have fun. And say happy birthday to Aunty from my side,' he replied groggily, woken up by my call.

'You don't have a problem with Sumer driving me down, right?' I shivered a little as I carefully asked him.

'Nope. Why would I? Have a good time. Even though I'd love a snuggle in this weather...but your family is important, so please go! And let me know once you reach Chandigarh.'

Around noon, just as I had finished packing, Sumer's name flashed on my cell phone, after more than a month. I answered the call.

'Hello...ummm...hi, Tanie.'

It felt strange, hearing your best friend take your name with the warmth of an acquaintance.

'Hi,' I replied, not knowing what else to say.

'I'm downstairs.'

'Okay. I'm coming.'

I glanced at myself in the mirror. Confident that I looked radiant despite being hungover, for I didn't want him to feel for even a second that I looked distraught without him. I locked the room, informed my PG landlady about my weekend plans and went out to his car. He got out on seeing me. I walked up to him. We shot each other an awkward look of acknowledgement.

It felt so different. Things had definitely changed. Sumer had definitely changed. For starters, he was wearing a well-fitting red sweater with a crisp white shirt, its collar folded over the V-neck of the sweater. And he was wearing clean ironed jeans. Then there were the black Wayfarers perched on his nose. He had cut his hair short and spiked it. And lost weight. A lot of it actually. But his forearms looked taut. And shoulders broader. Like he was on some lean muscle diet. His father would have been proud of him, if he were to see him right now. Maybe he had visited him. Or perhaps not. I wouldn't know.

We got confused between side-hugging and shaking hands. After an initial mix-up, we settled for the latter.

'Hi.'

'Hi.'

'You look...beautiful.'

'So do you…handsome, I mean.'

Okay, if the first five minutes were an indication, the next five hours were going to spell DISASTER.

I grabbed the heavy suitcase full of laundry that I had got and began to drag it to the boot of the car.

Even if I was just going back for the weekend, it obviously made sense to take the long-ignored laundry home and get it washed for free. I was a student in an alien city on a budget and I was entitled to little discounted joys in life.

'Ummm…give me the suitcase, I'll put it on the back seat.' Sumer lifted the suitcase as I struggled to drag it.

'No. It's okay.'

All this newborn formality. Strangulating.

He firmly took the suitcase from my hand and kept it on the back seat. 'Wow. What do you have in it? Are you not coming back to college on Monday?'

'Laundry,' I replied, looking at my feet.

He smiled. Very briefly. 'The boot is filled with mine as well. Always fun to take it for the mother to faint over. And who's going to pay for it here?'

The smile found a way to my face as well. We still thought alike. At least on some things. But the void of the last three months was too dark to fill with the brightness of just a smile.

We walked to the front of the car. And Sumer opened the door for me.

Clearly, a lot had changed.

He began to drive and we fell into a silence even more suffocating than the one you experience on a long flight. There at least you have a cute steward's dimple or a hot air hostess' smooth ass to ogle at when you're not sleepy.

Now if you thought about it, like deep down, Sumer and I hadn't really fought. And that's exactly where the problem lay.

When words that are meant to leave the body stay back, they create ulcers in the heart, and this damaged heart loses its ability to forget.

Our friendship had become diseased. And neither one of us wanted to see a doctor. Not yet.

We drove out of Delhi and got onto the highway. And just when I was about to choke on the silence, Sumer suddenly cleared his throat.

'You mind?' he said, putting a CD inside the music player.

'No.'

The music filled the car. A totally unfamiliar beat. Trance, perhaps. I reminded myself that his choices had changed. And my likes and dislikes didn't necessarily figure in them anymore. It felt disturbing. Even more than the music he had started to listen to. Unable to digest his newly acquired taste, I fished out my iPod and plugged in the earphones, turning my head away from him. He noticed, but didn't say anything.

We drove, listening to our own music, for another hour. Sure, we had a conversation, but it involved no words or smiles, only periodic quick and guilty glances.

Finally Sumer pulled into a petrol pump. And my bladder got activated as soon as it saw the washroom.

'I'll just go to the washroom and come back.'

'Okay.'

We got out of the car. Sumer got the car fuelled while I walked to the washroom. I let out a huge sigh of pent-up frustration as soon as I entered it. And got frustrated again almost immediately on seeing that the washroom door had a broken latch.

'Great. It just gets better with each passing second,' I muttered to myself as I opened the door again. There was no way I was peeing there. 'Fuck, you scared me,' I gasped.

Sumer was standing right at the door.

'Peeing is a birthright in a democracy.'

I tried hard not to smile. Especially as I was testing my bladder.

'The door doesn't have a latch. Anyhow, car key?' I extended my hand.

'Don't worry, I'll guard the door. Go,' he replied.

'It's okay. I'll pee later.'

He didn't need to take off his glasses for me to understand the look he gave me. We were driving on the highway. And peeing on the roadside wasn't exactly the best idea in an emergency situation, which would inevitably soon arise. I went back in and got down to my business.

'So how's Kabir?' Sumer spoke abruptly while I was still at it.

Just the place to finally have a conversation. Perfect.

'Good.' I paused. 'Actually, very good.' I smirked.

Tanie—1. Sumer—0.

He stayed silent.

'How's Liaka?' I asked him carefully, getting up from the pot.

'Good. It's like the best is happening to me all over again.'

He must have smirked outside.

Tanie—1. Sumer—1.

'How's college?' he asked.

'College is great. Good people, better times. Couldn't have asked for more.'

Tanie—2. Sumer—1.

So we were finally talking. In a public toilet. At a petrol pump. On a highway.

But at least we were talking.

'How's college?' I asked him.

'Good. Engineering clearly isn't the worst thing that has happened in my life recently. And it's been keeping Mom happy. My grades aren't the best but Dad just wants me to get through the year peacefully. Plus, I'm working on this movie—

Liaka's been a real help, and even the peeps at college have been really supportive. I'm happy to be doing mechanical engineering. At least I found reliable friends.'

Tanie—2. Sumer—10.

I had to counter that. Now! I opened the door. 'I'm sure. Hope your new friends don't end up dating someone you don't approve of.' Short. Sweet. Lethal.

Tanie—12. Sumer—10.

I walked to the car.

'Two thousand three hundred.' The guy who had fuelled our car was waiting.

Sumer came back and unlocked the car. We got in. Sumer paid the guy. I quickly took out my share of the money and kept it in the glass holder next to the gearbox. I knew that offering money for the fuel would piss him off further. The best friend Tanie wouldn't have done that. And I wasn't stopping at anything less than brutality.

'What's this?' Sumer said as he started the car.

'My share. You're driving me down, it's only fair that I pay my half. I don't want to feel the burden,' I said, plugging in my headphones again.

Sumer looked at me. No, wait, rather, he stared. A car pulled up behind us and started to honk.

'Drive?' I raised my eyebrows.

He angrily put the car into first gear and drove out of the pump rashly.

I smirked internally.

'A burden?' He accelerated further.

'Yes. You know...now that we aren't exactly...I mean...nothing.'

He opened his mouth to say something but stopped midway. He turned his concentration to the road, and the steadily rising speedometer began to worry me.

'Are you taking the cash back or not?' He put the car into fifth gear.

'Or you'll kill us?' I said bravely, despite shitting bricks deep down. He was driving really fast, even for a highway.

There was a time when we would give birth to long, serpentine queues at the paid parking lots while arguing over who would pay the five rupees for the parking ticket, as the parking guy would abuse us under his breath. Or how we tried making sure during the interval of a movie that the other paid for the popcorn and Coke, by faking an urgent toilet call. Or how we would simply steal money from each other's wallets, for cheap thrills.

'I won't kill us, Tanie, you've killed "us" already. By not trusting me over that Kabir.'

'What do you mean?'

'Oh c'mon, like you don't know what I mean, Tanie. The last three months—you've behaved like I don't exist.'

He overtook a car from the wrong lane.

'Have I? How am I supposed to behave with you if you don't answer my calls?'

'That was just that one time.'

He narrowly cut off another car.

'And you start dating that bitch Liaka! Without even asking me.'

'That's my girlfriend you're talking about. Mind your tongue, you're no less of a…'

The tempers and the acceleration rose. In equal measure. Scarily.

'Call me a bitch, na! Just say it… You're dating the same girl who you thought was an easy lay and today you're all protective about her…I'm sure you love her now. Sex is all about love, isn't it?' The sarcasm dripped from my tongue.

'Yup. Funny how someone who goes about kissing her

ex-boyfriend, drunk, in a club, has something to say about me. And then the same person meets a random dude in a washroom and the next thing you know, she's doing him. Oh…I forgot…your first time has to be special…I'm sure, Virgin Mary!'

Those words stung. 'Stop the car,' I shouted. 'Stop the car!' I repeated, when he didn't comply. 'Sumer,' I said. 'STOP THE FUCKING CAR!'

I don't know what made me do it. But I did it.

I pulled the handbrake. And Sumer, the car's wheels and I squealed in horror as the car skid. He tried really hard not to get us killed as he dodged other cars on the road, his foot stuck to the brakes, hands trying hard not to let the steering wheel spin out of control.

We went off the road and ended up ramming his car into the rear of a stationary Innova.

The word ulcers had finally cleared. Just that we were in an accident.

And accidents are never rosy.

'Tanie?'

I was too horrified and stunned to react to what had just happened. Sumer had put all his effort into making sure the car's momentum slowed, yet even then, the inertia or whatever jazz they had taught us in physics in class ten meant that though our car just kissed the rear-end of the Innova, both cars were damaged.

And the first proof of it was the smoke rising out of the engine of Sumer's car.

Sumer! I turned around to look at him. He was coughing. And massaging his chest. But apart from that, he looked just about fine. His glasses had come off and I saw his eyes. And the trauma of what had just happened was reflected in them.

'Tanie, are you fine?'

'Yeah,' I groaned.

'Here.' Sumer unbuckled what had saved me from banging my head into the windshield. And him, for that matter. The seatbelt.

'Feeling better?' He hesitated for a moment, then inched forward and hugged me.

It felt better. Much better. I hugged him back.

'*B***chod…come out, you phucker!*'

Turns out we had forgotten that we had rammed into another car. And it wasn't exactly unoccupied, even though it was randomly parked alongside the road. A burly driver with a big paunch was trying his best to open Sumer's door, abusing at the top of his voice.

Sumer gave me a look that I feared and understood.

'No,' I murmured.

'Yes!'

'No, Sumer.'

'Tanie. Cops. Drama. Your mom's surprise party!'

He turned the key. The fat driver froze on hearing the engine's noise. Even he knew what was coming. The sound of abuses, plastic, metal, screeching tyres and honking all mixed up as Sumer reversed the car at full throttle.

We heard our Swift's bumper crack as Sumer tried to pull away from the boot of the Innova.

I looked at the damage our damaged friendship had caused to the fat driver's car. His left tail light was broken. And the boot would need a session of intense denting and painting.

'Sumer, watch out!'

The driver had picked up a small stone and stood blocking our way. A car or two was also beginning to slow down, to enjoy the free drama. Or perhaps to help the Innova driver and make sure we went behind bars.

'Fuck this shit!' Sumer shouted as he accelerated the car.

The bumper threatened to give way from one side; with it touching the front tyre, Sumer narrowly avoided the driver, whose reflexes weren't as bold as his appetite.

We got back on the road and Sumer drove like a maniac, giving the driver no chance of following us. The driver didn't even have the time to take down the licence plate number of Sumer's car, for no cop followed us or intercepted us at the police nakas. Yet, to be completely sure that we didn't get into any type of trouble, we didn't stop anywhere till we reached Chandigarh. Not even for lunch, even though Sumer insisted I eat. Or for peeing. Which I hoped he would insist on.

Around 5 in the evening, Sumer stopped his car a little before my house. I had already checked with Dad—Mom and Aarti aunty were at the spa and wouldn't return before 8.30 p.m. I could enter the house and help Dad.

We both got out of the car. I got my bag out and walked up to Sumer, who was busy inspecting the damage. And possibly thinking what he would tell his mother when she saw the car.

'The bumper's gone. The bonnet needs a little touch-up as well. Oh man!' he commented as he scraped off the already peeling paint.

'I'll pay for it.' The words came out involuntarily this time.

'Tanie—' Sumer looked at me.

The last time I had used those very words, we had almost died.

'I mean…I genuinely mean it,' I said defensively.

A smile broke out on Sumer's face. And I realized he wasn't angry.

'Tan Tan…just go inside before your dad comes out. I'll take the car to the mechanic and try to make it look a little more presentable so that Mom doesn't die thinking I get into accidents every day and doesn't let me take the car back to Delhi.'

'I'm sorry, Sumer.'

'Don't be, I'll send you the bill. Obviously.'

I smiled.

'I genuinely mean it. I'm using the money you put near the gearbox and I'll tell you the balance amount that needs to be paid. And I don't expect to be reimbursed in kind.' He touched his crotch. 'This one's doing fine. So you're paying in cash.'

Pure, classic, vintage Sumer.

'Okay.' I smiled and started to walk towards my house.

'Tanie,' Sumer shouted when I was at the gate.

'Yeah?' I walked back a few steps.

'So do I have a best friend again?'

My phone rang just then. I stared at the screen.

'Hi, Kabir. I'll…I'll talk to you in a bit.' I cut the call.

Only to find Sumer had already gotten into the car. Without listening to my reply.

I sighed.

'My father is having an affair. And I think Mom knows and that's why he's doing all of this…my parents are getting divorced! I'll be a troubled child.'

Earlier in the evening, I had entered the house to find a canopy being erected to cover the garden. And a slew of people, ranging from caterers to decorators, being ordered around by Reena, my 'empowered' maid, and my frantic dad. The DJ was setting up his own space. Mom would be back from the spa by 8.30 and the guests were going to arrive by 8.

'My sexy drama queen, your father is just trying to make your mom feel special. I think he's being a true gentleman.'

Kabir looked so edible in his gym vest. I was in my room, getting ready and Facetiming with him.

'What's that on your neck?' My eyes suddenly focused on a mark.

'What...this?' he touched the reddened spot. 'Oh, that's a hickey. I just got laid.'

'Very funny.'

'I'm not joking,' he said in a serious tone.

'Okay. I need to go, it's 7.45...the guests will arrive soon.' I was about to cut the call when he stopped me.

'I was lifting, Tanie. Wait.' He walked out to his workout room. 'See?' He placed the phone so I could see him lift a weight bar. He came back and showed me his neck again; it was reddened on the other side.

'Sorry,' I said guiltily.

'It's cool. I like the possessive bit. Makes for great action. Whenever we do it,' he said casually.

'Kabir...'

'Hmm?'

'Thanks for not pushing me into doing it.'

'I like the fact that you want your first time to be so special, Tanie. It makes you all the more desirable and makes me feel all the more lucky to have you.'

I planted a kiss on the front camera of my mobile.

'Tanie, are you ready?'

The mobile fell out of my hand. And luckily Kabir cut the call. Dad had walked into the room. He was wearing a blue shirt that Mom had gifted him but he had never gotten around to appreciate by wearing.

'Okay, hurry. And call Sumer, please. I've been trying to get through to his number...'

'Sumer...why?' I asked, confused.

'Because...' my dad began and then stopped. 'You'll know.

Just come down and welcome the guests, they will be here soon. And when your mother's relatives come, I don't want to be alone.' He left.

I called Kabir back, who reassured me that I was looking pretty in my woollen skirt and overcoat, and walked out to the garden.

My house looked beautiful. And smelled yummy. Almost making me regret not wanting to stay in Chandigarh for college. But then I wouldn't have met Kabir, or my friends at college, or had the fun that I had had. And lost Sumer...

'Sumer!' my dad exclaimed as I saw Sumer pull in a projector screen on wheels.

'Tanie, give him a hand,' Dad ordered.

'Yes...yes...' I stirred and went to help him.

'Why have you got this screen? And what about the car?' I darted questions at Sumer awkwardly as Dad guided us while we positioned the screen.

Sumer had changed and looked even smarter in a black overcoat and formal pants. This bitch Liaka had clearly done some good in his life.

Sumer just smiled back at me. His eyes were bloodshot again.

'Have you been drinking?' I asked him after Dad went to greet a guest who had actually arrived on time.

Sumer looked at me. 'No, Tanie, I've not taken off my lenses. And the car is fine. He couldn't repair it so soon. But it's okay. Mom won't freak out. I just hope she doesn't tell Dad though. Thank God he's fighting Somalian pirates as we speak.' He smiled. 'And I took the liberty of informing Stuti about tonight...coz she told me you hadn't...but she can't make it, she's not in town...I'm assuming you got too busy with Uncle—and other "things"—to inform your friend that you're in town and have a party at home.'

Fuck. I had forgotten to call Stuti! Kabir had taken up all my time, ever since I had come home this evening.

'Sumer...' I began, but then Dad called me. Mom's relatives had arrived and he needed a peacekeeping force to stop him from starting the war, as usual.

Scented aunties, bored uncles, lusty-for-free-alcohol teenagers, quite a few family friends—some whom I liked and some I did not—arrived soon after.

I jumped from one group to the other, making sure the guests got fed and stimulated enough till Mom arrived. Sumer, on the other hand, was already at the bar, drinking secretly and talking to some guy he knew from his school. I so needed a drink myself but considering this was my house and my party, and even one drink here could cause a volcanic explosion, I refrained.

'Everyone...she's going to be here in a minute,' Dad announced on a microphone. He had a glass of Scotch in his hand, which he chugged.

I wanted to pull his cheeks. So much preparation!

Mom's car pulled into the driveway the next minute.

'SURPRISE!' everyone shouted. The DJ played a 'Happy Birthday' track.

Mom stepped out of the car, shell-shocked. I walked up to Dad. Aarti aunty escorted my mom to the little dance floor the DJ had created. Mom saw me, then Dad, and a tear rolled down her cheek.

Dad took Mom's hand in his.

'This is beautiful,' she whispered.

'It hasn't even started yet.' Dad winked.

This was love. In its most parental form.

Dad raised a thumb and I followed his line of vision to see Sumer sitting on his haunches, with his laptop connected to a projector.

The screen that Sumer had rolled in earlier lit up with his laptop's homepage. And behind the few desktop icons that appeared was an old picture of us. Both of us in our school uniforms at the laser tag in the mall. Not many noticed it. But Sumer and I did. And our eyes connected for a moment. I swallowed the lump in my throat. He still missed me. I still missed him.

Sumer looked away and a video started on the projector screen.

'One day you'll be old.'

Everyone hooted and I looked at the screen, surprised. It was Dad's voice, supported by a video shot of an old man's hand running over a golf set. With soft music adding the finer touches in the background.

'And I'll still disturb your sleep as I go to play golf every morning.' A shot of the same old man, his face hidden, towering over his old wife and shaking her.

'You'll curse me before you put on those artificial teeth.' A quick shot of a woman's back, dissolving to a wrinkled hand as the silhouette of the old man walks away.

'And we'll fight, like any other morning.' The next shot was of two cups of tea, first being filled and then falling to the floor and breaking. Dramatic music in support. *'You'll clean the mess.'* A walking stick, broken china and the same old lady bending down, tired, to clean it up.

'While I create some more for you.' A shot of the old man at a golf range as he stepped in a puddle and soiled his socks.

'And I'll come back and you'll still meet me with a smile.' A door opening, with a bolt of sunshine, welcoming the man's silhouette.

'While I walk past you.' A tight, close shot of the man's and the woman's shoulders brushing.

'You've given me everything.' A montage of pictures, of Mom

and Dad getting married, of them on their honeymoon, with me, our house, our dog Liaka, vacations—all the old memories.

'And I've given you nothing.' An old video recording that I had shot, of Dad looking away as Mom was calling out to him.

'I've often taken you for granted and you've never complained.' A picture of Mom smiling.

'But today I want to let you know that I'm going to start afresh.' The screen went black and then suddenly Dad appeared on it, in the same clothes that he was wearing that evening.

He spoke, 'Smiley...stop crying.' I looked at Mom in real time as she smiled and wiped her tears. Dad, as if knowing Mom would do just that, took out a tissue in the video and continued, 'You must be surprised, or rather, shocked, at what you've been seeing. Well, it's your birthday and you deserve to know this...last week, remember when we fought, when I woke you up because I couldn't find my car key and you shouted at me and I left for the club and came back with a damaged car? I lied to you about the accident. I told you I didn't know who banged into the car in the parking lot of the golf club as I was on the course. But the truth is that I was very much there when the accident took place. I was standing just next to the car when a kid lost control of his car and made us poorer.' An image of our damaged car, about which I wasn't even informed, flashed on the screen and then dissolved, just as quickly. Dad appeared on the screen again.

'Well, I had a very narrow escape. And that day itself I decided I would do something special for you on your birthday.' The music in the video stopped. Dad spoke again, in the video, with emotion in his voice, 'Smiley, Tanie and all the beautiful people in my life...that moment I realized that life is too unpredictable to fight with the people you consider your companions, just because they don't like something you love. Love them for who they are, not what they choose. Because perfection is plastic and imperfection makes relationships real. If we accept unabashed love from the people we love, why can't we accept the pain that they give us too?

Sumer and I looked at each other again. This was for us.

'Happy birthday.' The video ended. And the end credits rolled. With Sumer's name listed. And in that moment I realized that Sumer had painstakingly made the video at Dad's behest. This despite us not exactly being the bum chums that we were earlier.

Sumer was special. Way too special. And losing him over an inflated ego was the stupidest thing that I could do. He wasn't just a friend. He wasn't my lover. He was special. And no social mores could define what we shared.

I looked at Sumer, who was also teary-eyed, seeing his name scroll down the screen.

His dream.

Everyone began to clap. The DJ put the spotlight on Mom and Dad. And they weren't the only ones with tears in their eyes. There also stood Aarti aunty who had seen Sumer's work with the camera. A guilty tear rolled down her cheek as she saw her son living a reality he had chosen for his mother's happiness. Everyone continued to clap like crazy. Sumer walked up to Aarti aunty and wiped her tears.

'You've done an amazing job with the video, Sumer. I love you, beta. And I'm sorry.' Aarti aunty's voice reached my ears.

'I like what I'm doing, Ma. Don't cry. Four years to Dad's dream and then it's my vision,' I heard him tell her.

I was about to go and hug him for making this day so special for my parents, for his mother, for just being...HIM...when Dad called me and embraced me in a family hug.

When I managed to wriggle out of it, Sumer wasn't around. I walked up to his mom frantically. 'Aunty, where's Sumer?'

'He's gone home for a while, beta. He told me he wasn't feeling well.'

I sneaked out of the party. Dad and Mom were too drained by emotion to notice. There was no way I wasn't going to talk to him. I walked to his house, entered, went up to his room and opened the door, without asking for permission.

'Dhillon, I'll cut your balls! What drama are—' I stopped as I saw him curled up in a corner. I walked up to him and sat down on the floor. He looked up at me with bloodshot eyes. Like he had been crying. His right hand kept shaking a little. I held it.

'Are you okay?'

Sumer kept staring at me without saying anything. Like he was in a trance. Then he just hugged me. And I hugged him back. Like we were making up for all the lost time.

'Do you want a drink?' Sumer suddenly asked me and broke the embrace.

'Um. Yeah. Okay,' I said, confused. I had to get back to the party before Mom and Dad realized I was gone.

Sumer came back with a quarter of vodka from his cupboard and poured it into a mug. He took a sip, neat, and offered me the mug. I followed suit. We drained the quarter quickly, without talking much. And got tipsy even faster.

Sumer cleared his throat. 'My mother's fucked-up husband didn't let me make movies, Tanie. You saw how bloody good I am at it. And then, you bitch...you don't have time for me now because you have a boyfriend whom I don't like.'

Just like old times.

'Sumer, I know you bloody well care about me. You wouldn't do something so beautiful for my parents otherwise. And it's only fair if you think that Kabir isn't a good guy, but that doesn't change the truth, right? I've missed you so much in these last three months. I've missed you every time I've wanted to crack a dirty joke, I've missed you every time I've wanted to listen to the latest gossip, I've missed you every time I've wanted to go to a mall drunk and play air hockey, I've missed you every time I wanted to just go out in my boxer shorts and drink cheap port wine. Kabir is a wonderful guy, he keeps me very happy but I've missed you…I've missed life…I've missed my best friend. Let's just start over. Let's become the old Sumer and Tanie.'

Sumer suddenly began to unzip his pants.

'Dude!' I shouted.

'You wanted us to become the old Sumer and Tanie. How can you forget we had comfort sex every night?' He ran his hand over my thigh.

'Yuck.' I slapped his hand.

'What? Don't act like you haven't missed this.' He touched my lips.

I bit his finger.

'Aaoww!'

I let go. 'Yes. I've been a dry desert without you,' I said in fake seduction.

'Yeah? Well then, let me see.'

Sumer and I wrestled. With a restored vengeance. He tried hard to overpower me but I fought back in equal measure.

My phone rang and he got off me. It was Dad.

'Let's go. Dad's calling.'

We got up. Sumer pulled me back into a hug.

'Welcome back, Tan Tan.'

'Welcome back, Summu.'

'By the way, I stole the vodka that we had from your dad's bar, sometime ago.'

'You're cheap.'

'That I am. And that's why we are best friends.'

He smiled. She smiled. Problem solved.

7 January 2014

Ambience Mall, Vasant Kunj
Inside Zara
2.14 p.m.

'So…how do they look?'
　'Great. Can we go eat now, I'm hungry.'
　'No, wait! I think I like the black trousers better. Give me two minutes.'
Five minutes later.
'So?'
'So?'
'I'm still confused…black or blue?'
'Can I be honest? I GENUINELY don't care. We've been here for the last thirty minutes! And I'm starving.'
'Okay…okay…I think I'm done… Can you just get me a waist size 31 in the white pants that we saw earlier? I don't think either of these highlight my workout butt.'
'Jesus! You're so annoying.'
Five minutes later.
'Here.'
'Easy. You don't have to throw them at me.'
'M***…fucker.'
At the cash counter.
'Sir, ma'am.'
'Yes. When does your summer collection come out?'
'Umm…in the summer.'
'Jesus! This blonde.'
'That'll be two thousand nine hundred.'
Silence.
'Two thousand nine hundred, sir.'
'Oh, me? No, ma'am's paying.'
'Give us two minutes…'

'What? Stop pulling me by my ears, people are watching.'

'They were also watching you at your gay best when you took thirty minutes to buy those pants… And when does the summer collection come out? Seriously, Sumer!'

'Oh c'mon, Tanie, a man has needs. And Liaka loves my butt. Only if she is happy will she make me happy.'

'You're disgusting. Why the fuck do I pay for you?'

'Cause you almost got us killed last month. It's called collateral damage.'

'You're incorrigible.'

'Okay, now I'm hungry. Can we please leave?'

'You know, and I say this with all my heart, life would have been much better if I had branched out a few years ago and made more friends.'

'Ma'am…two thousand nine hundred.'

'Yes, I'm paying!'

'I love you, Tan Tan.'

'Whore.'

'Bitch.'

'Slut.'

'Slut's best friend.'

He smiled. She smiled. Problem solved.

28 January 2014

WhatsApp conversation, around 5.45 p.m.

Tanie   Are you sure we should do this?
Sumer   Yes, Tanie. I think it's time.
Tanie   Sumer, I know Kabir is going to love the idea...but you...are you sure you'll be okay with it? And what about Liaka?
Sumer   Oh yes, I think it's going to be a crazy experience. All of us need to get to know each other better and what better way than by doing it together! I've already asked Liaka. She thinks it's going to be fun. The four of us...together...all the adrenaline...the speed...the thrill...let's do this shit.
Tanie   Okay, Kabir says it's on. What time?
Sumer   Around 1 a.m.?
Tanie   Won't that be too late?
Sumer   Tanie, the darker it is, the lesser chances of getting caught.
Tanie   Cool. See you tonight. This is going to be my first time.
Sumer   If this goes well, Kabir and I could actually become friends.
Tanie   Fingers crossed.

The next afternoon

Sumer Morning, Tan Tan! Last night was crazy.
Tanie Yeah. Sure was.
Sumer Kabir's a nice guy.
Tanie Yeah? Do you really mean it?
Sumer Yes…we should totally do this again.
Tanie NO. I almost puked last night.
Sumer Oh c'mon…CAR RACING is so much fun! Especially when you're doing it on the Jaipur highway and you beat your best friend's boyfriend at it. Ha, so much for being a professional F1 racer.
Tanie You JUST said you liked him!
Sumer Haha. Chill. We should all go clubbing sometime.
Tanie Yeah, Liaka and I need to connect as well.
Sumer I love you, Tan Tan. Come now, I have a morning hard-on. Wait, I'll just Snapchat a picture to you.

Tanie Bye.	
Sumer I love you.	
Tanie I know.	

3 March 2014

Inside the girls' washroom at LAP—the club
1.35 a.m.

Two drunk girls. One cubicle.
   <sounds of puking>
   'Shhh…it's okay…take it easy…here, take a tissue, Liaka.'
   'Thanks, Tanie…oh fuckkkk…' *<pukes>*
   'It's okay…it's okay… Here, let me help you.'
   'Ah. Fuck, that's a lot of puke.'
   'Um. Yes.'
   Five minutes later. At the washbasin.
   'I generally don't do this. I'm sorry.'
   'I know, Liaka. You don't have to be sorry.'
   'No, Tanie, I'm sorry for what I did to you at my house. And I'm not saying this coz I'm really drunk and at my honest best…I was…I was just jealous of you. I was the most important person in Sumer's life before you came on the scene, and I just couldn't take it. So when the break-up happened, I conveniently put the blame on you in my head.'
   'That…that's…thanks, Liaka. I hope you know you're prettier than I can be even on my best hair day. And I'm not saying this coz I'm really drunk as well.'

'Okay, now this is getting to be too much of a lesbian moment.'

'Yeah. You do have a flat chest though, Liaka.'

'And you're fucking tiny. I'm sure all Kabir has to do is to stand up and unbuckle, right, Tanie?'

'Um—'

'Um—'

'We're drunk. Let's stop.'

Awkward silence.

'Do you have some gloss, Tanie? I smudged my lipstick completely.'

'Sure. One minute…here you go.'

'Great, we shared cosmetics, we're friends again.'

'Er…yes…Liaka…do you really like Sumer?'

'I do, Tanie. More than ever now.'

'He really likes you. And I'm not sure how I would react if I saw him sad again. So you get the drift, right?'

'I do.'

'Okay then, let's go and drink to a new friendship.'

'But before that, let's click a mirror selfie, the lighting in here is amazing.'

Meanwhile, outside, at the bar.
The best friend. The boyfriend.

'Two Black Labels. 30 ml. Soda. Ice.'

'Sir.'

'Hey hey…Kabir…I'm paying.'

'It's cool, Sumer.'

'Give that card back to him. You got us on the guest list. Drinks on me.'

'Sir.'

'Here, your card and your drink.'
Glasses picked up and raised to each other, in acknowledgment. Alcohol in the system.
'Kabir, you know I've always wondered, what do these girls do in the washroom?'
'I hear there are sofas inside to chill and gossip. And obviously a make-up vending machine. And maybe rooms for some girl-on-girl action.'
Chauvinistic laughter.
'In that case, Kabir, I suggest we go.'
'After you, sir.'
Some more alcohol. Some more laughter.
'Kabir, you're actually not that bad.'
'Sumer, will you blow me next?'
'Haha. No man, you're a good guy. Tanie is really into you. And anything that makes her happy makes me happy.'
'She loves it when I kiss her. Where does that leave us now?'
'Dude. You're creeping me out.'
'Haha. Don't worry, Sumer…I know you mean the best for her.'
'I do. Trust me when I say this, you do anything wrong with her and I will kick your balls so hard…'
'I get the drift, Sumer. Another drink?'
'Sure.'

An hour later.
Waiting for the valet.
'Thanks, Sumer. Kabir says you're a good guy.'
'That's what I think about myself too, Tanie.'
'Shut up.'
'Liaka likes you as well.'

'She doesn't have a choice.'
'Shut up.'
He smiled. She smiled. Problem solved.

17 April 2014

Sumer's house. The living room. Movie night.
9.45 p.m.

'It's been thirty minutes. You're supposed to give us free pizza now.'

'No, sir. It's been twenty-nine minutes. You can check the bill.'

'I will not check the bill. You're late and that's final. My father is a lawyer…I swear I'll go to the consumer court. It's not about the money, it's about integrity.'

'Sir…sir…please, sir.'

'Don't mind him, he was born cheap. What's the total?'

'Eight hundred and forty-two, ma'am.'

'Great.'

A girl's hand. A boy's pocket. And some movement.

'Ah…that feels good…don't take your hand out from my pocket…oh…Tanie…don't stop.'

Embarrassed pizza guy. And a wallet thus procured.

'There you go. Keep the change.'

The door is shut.

'You're such a bitch.'

'I like your wallet, Sumer. Nice and empty.'

Forty minutes, six Chicken Supreme slices, four beers, one unaccounted-for fart, three loud burps and two yawns later.

'Argh.'

'Aye…why did you stop the movie, Sumer?'

'Its bloody boring, Tanie!'

'It's *Sherlock Holmes*. You're a guy, you're supposed to like all of this stuff.'

'I don't. I told you to rent something like *The Ugly Truth*...like a nice rom-com or some animated movie. You should have totally downloaded *Frozen*, I heard it's really nice.'

'Aww...my princess.'

'Don't pull my cheeks!'

'Haha. C'mon, let's forward the movie to a sex scene for you.'

'No!'

'Sumer, you're saying "no" to this offer! All good?'

'Haha. Yes, Tanie, all's good. I get enough of it from Liaka. These videos don't do it for me anymore. But obviously you wouldn't know.'

'What do you mean?'

'Haha...you know what I mean, Tan Tan. But fuck it; oops, I forgot you don't like to "fuck it".'

An angry pillow thrown. A dirty look shot. Two more beer bottles opened. Legs curled up on the sofa. And a silence, just broken.

'For someone who is willing to hump anything that moves, the concept of waiting for the right time would obviously sound alien.'

'Tanie! Tanie! Tanie!'

'Don't touch me. You just scratched your balls.'

'Oooh, you noticed that. You're clearly deprived.'

'I'm not, Sumer. Kabir and I do what it takes to, you know...'

'I know?'

'Make it worth what it's worth.'

'Oh c'mon, Tanie, haven't you heard the saying... If you don't go all the way, you don't make any hay.'

'Huh?'

'Listen. I won't judge you on this. But is Kabir a guy? Like, a man?'

Balls scratched again. To signify intention. Piercing feminine eyes, not moving from the crotch. In retaliation. Like they mean what they say.

'Yeah. He's a real man. Unlike the boys in my life.'

'Come touch my boy then.'

'You're disgusting.'

'Haha. But Tanie, seriously, let's get this straight. You've been dating him for around eight months now? And you've not yet sealed the deal…and if he really is twenty-two and not homo, he has to be cheating on you.'

'You know, that's why he is a man. And I've seen and felt him enough to know that. He understands that I'm not ready yet and the day I am…we'll make love. And not have sex.'

'Hahahahhahahaha!'

'Fuck you.'

A manly voice in a feminine imitation. 'We'll make love. And not have sex.'

'Screw you, Sumer! Just because that Liaka is a horny bitch.'

'Aye! She's just a good girlfriend.'

'And so is Kabir.'

'I'm sure he is, Tanie.'

Twenty awkward minutes later. I'm unsettled. Clouded thoughts. He is busy finding a new movie to watch from his collection on the laptop.

'Sumer?'

'Hmmm.'

'Is there any way…I can make him feel…you know…surprise him with something more…'

'Pleasurable?'

'Shut up.'

'Yes you can, Tan Tan. You want me to show you?'
'No!'
'C'mon...'
'Keep your hands off me or you know what I'm capable of doing.'
'No, not the balls again!'
'Haha.'
'So yes, Tanie Brar, you can make your boyfriend "happy". Have you tried the earlobe trick?'
'Yup.'
'The ball tickle?'
'Yup.'
'Talking dirty?'
'Yup.'
'Role play?'
'Yup.'
'Dry humping?'
'Yup.'
'Back massage?'
'Yup.'
'Footsie?'
'Yup.'
'God, my best friend is a closet slut.'
'Hahaha.'
'Seriously, teach Liaka something. Be of some use, Tanie.'
'Sure.'
'Or maybe...'
'Stop unzipping your pants!'
'I thought you were drunk. Okay just flash na, once. You know how Liaka is...'
'Flat?'
'Oi...actually...yes.'
'All you'll get is this...'

A kiss on the cheek. Two best friends.
He smiled. She smiled. Problem solved.

16 May 2014

My room.
EXAMS!
3 a.m.

'SUMER! If I'm not taking your calls, there has to be a goddamn reason. Will you let me study in peace?'

'Please don't shout. I'm dying.'

'Good for you. Now bye.'

A cut call. An angry yawn. And just when you get back to the books...

'Sumer. You call me again and I'll kill you.'

'Please do that, Tanie. I'm flunking tomorrow anyway. Vikram will come home next month and murder me when he sees my first-year results. I should have taken engineering more seriously.'

'It's too late for realization. Now call Liaka and PMS, okay?'

'I did. Before calling you. She's switched off her phone now.'

'Haha. So much for being a girlfriend.'

'That's why you're my best friend.'

'Shut up. You've hardly been in touch the last few days.'

'That's because I was studying, Tanie.'

'Okay Sumer, let's get back to work.'

'Um...'

'Now what?'

A loud screech in the background. Heard on the phone. And on the road. Outside my window!

'SUMER, where are you?'
'Um…outside your house.'
'Doing what exactly?'
'Let's go to Paharganj for a drink? Or to the border? I couldn't sleep. Jump over the gate, we'll come back soon.'
'ARE YOU CRAZY?'
'You remember the rule, right? If we go down, we go down in style.'
A guilty look at the books. A confused mind.
'No.'
'I heard a yes.'
'No, Sumer.'
'Yes, Tan Tan. I know you can do with a drink too.'
'Grrr…why did I become your best friend?'
'Because you're as fucked up as I am?'
'Just one drink.'
'That's what she said.'
He smiled. She smiled. Problem solved.

Exams got over by May-end. And the realization dawned that we would have to go back to Chandigarh for the summer holidays. Leaving behind Delhi, our friends, Liaka and Kabir. Funnily enough, Sumer didn't take to the temporary separation well. He actually cried over being away from Liaka. I was relatively more sorted in the head for Kabir was anyhow going to Europe with his friends. *Zindagi Na Milegi Dobara* had released in 2011 and they had experienced a late awakening. Sumer had told me to 'seal the deal' with Kabir before he left for greener and whiter pastures and I almost gave in, only to panic at the last moment. Guilty, I even thought of giving him a free pass but then common sense took centre stage and I allowed him to go to a strip club. And never mention it to me in any of our conversations.

We arrived home. Both our mothers shrieked on seeing how thin we had both become. And that's when I actually realized that Sumer had lost more weight in the last four months. The veins in his arms were visible and his body had lost a lot of mass, despite the fact that he ate like a pig all the time.

'It's called circuit training. Google it.' He collectively shut all the ladies up.

In June, the entire gang from school—Megha (with an accent), Stuti, Viraaj, Shiven, Sumer and I finally had our reunion.

We met at this sports bar called Underdoggs. Initially we ran out of conversation. But once we realized it was happy hour and they had some amazing beer towers, everything fell into place. Shared stories turned into serious revelations of the past year as the alcohol kept coming.

Megha had made out with a married guy. Stuti had started smoking (I cringed at that). Shiven, who was once again holding hands with Megha under the table, had passed out in a public washroom. Viraaj had had a fling with a twenty-nine-year-old woman in Mumbai.

Everyone had got fucked up in some manner. And we all drank to that. Happily. Not just that night, but for the entire time we were home. Now that all of us were successfully in college, our parents didn't exactly die of anxiety attacks as we partied almost every second night. They probably suspected our drinking habits but none of us ever had that dinner-table conversation with them. Neither did the parents stop us from going clubbing officially.

Most surprisingly, even Sumer's dad, who came back around the same time, didn't give him a very hard time. The only complaint he had was with his weight. In fact, he approved of

Sumer's newly acquired sense of dressing. Just like I had guessed he would.

I did miss Kabir and we often talked. So did Sumer and Liaka. In fact, he even drove down to Delhi to meet her three or four times. I accompanied him on two trips and met my college friends.

After one of the trips he took alone he came back with a necklace of hickeys and I applied an entire bottle of concealer on his neck so that his father wouldn't notice.

Our exam results came out in July and I did reasonably well. Even Sumer cleared all his exams and his father, though not pleased, didn't beat him either.

July ended. The gang bid a tearful goodbye to each other. Promising we would be better at keeping in touch, knowing it wasn't going to happen beyond the second weekend.

We came back to Delhi. I met Kabir again. We made out like crazy. Sumer dug Liaka. And told me he had tried a new position with her.

In late August, I finally decided that I was going to take my relationship to the next level with Kabir, on our first anniversary, the following month. I even went lingerie shopping for the occasion. With Sumer, and his lusty tongue hanging out of his mouth, in tow.

But then, life is what happens to you when you're planning other things. Or some fucked-up jazz that they say about it.

And life happened to us on Liaka's birthday, exactly two weeks before I had decided to 'seal the deal'.

If only Sumer hadn't done it, things wouldn't have changed. And the good life would have continued.

If only.

4 September 2014

Sumer's house
8.45 p.m.

'Why don't you wear that shirt?'

'Huh?' Sumer stood bare-chested, in his boxers, clueless. A look of worry etched on his face.

Liaka was celebrating her birthday at Kitty Su later that night. Sumer had called me earlier in the evening to ask me to come to his house and help him get ready like a boss, to which I had readily agreed. He had a huge mirror and a nice shower in his apartment, unlike my depressing PG, and Kabir was going to join us directly at the club, for he had a wedding to attend before that.

'Listen, stop acting like a girl; whatever you wear, Liaka will want to strip it off you soon after, so chill!' I said.

He didn't smile.

'Sumer, I need to get ready as well, so stop fretting like a girl.'

He looked away.

Okay, something was definitely bothering him. In fact, he had been distracted ever since he had opened the door for me.

I walked up to him. 'Dhillon, people in Somalia are dying of hunger and you can't decide what shirt to wear tonight? First-world issue much?'

He smiled absent-mindedly.

'Do you want a pad, since you won't stop with your mood swings?' Another joke fallen flat. 'Okay, now you're scaring me.'

'Tanie…let's drink. I have some vodka.' He didn't wait for me to protest and walked out of his room.

Confused, I followed him to the living room, where he had already poured two large vodka-Cokes for us. His cook looked on from the kitchen. And from his perspective, there was a boxer-clad Sumer with the Didi who would come often to the house and drink. He smirked. And I hated it.

'Sumer—'

'Here.' He thrust the glass in my hand.

'I don't want to drink.'

He chugged his drink. And started to cough.

I rubbed his back. 'Okay now, Dhillon, enough! Tell me, what's up?'

'Tanie…I…last week…so…last week, Liaka came over and we got really drunk. And…I…we…I mean…I…it's all so fucked up…how do I say this? I don't know why I didn't tell you this earlier…' A pregnant pause. Long enough to give birth to my worst fear.

'She's late! And you were too drunk to remember if you used protection or not? And you told her you used protection, to safeguard yourself?'

Boys.

He just stared blankly at me. Neither confirming nor denying my statement. I gulped down my drink. I needed it now.

He looked down.

Confirmation.

'Has she taken a test?'

I poured myself another drink.

'You want some Coke with it?' he asked in a small voice.

'FUCK YOU, Sumer! For all you know, you're on your way to fathering a child and you're concerned about getting me Coke for my drink? Have you lost it? She needs to take the test…she can't just ignore it. And you can't be so irresponsible!'

He looked at me, embarrassed, as he quickly poured another drink for himself and chugged it down.

I took a deep fortifying breath. Like the ones you take before approaching your history book the night before the exam.

'Okay, so we don't ruin her birthday night. Tomorrow morning we make her take the test. And we act normally tonight, okay? It's her birthday.'

'Hmm.'

'Fuck you, Sumer, I can't believe you'd do this to a girl. What if Kabir did this to me?' I walked off with my drink to the guest room and shut the door with a bang, to let him know how disappointed I was in him.

The vodka did its trick. Two neat shots and I got ready in a buzzed trance. Sumer very well knew that if he wanted to make sure I didn't cut his balls off and burn them on a simmering gas flame, he would have to adulterate my bloodstream, and he had very cleverly done just that.

'Let's go.' I tried hard to maintain my balance in my heels and the anger in my eyes as I walked out to him.

'Okay.'

He had a vacant look in his eyes and they were on the borderline of looking bloodshot again. Like he had finished the vodka bottle in my absence.

We drove to Kitty Su, with rock music and the silence between us for company. Liaka had put our names down on the guest list. That too for the VIP area.

We entered the club and made our way to the VIP area.

'Baby!' Liaka hugged Sumer. Excitedly. And then started to lick his neck.

'Happy birthday, Liaka.' I quickly reminded her that they weren't exactly alone.

We side-hugged. She smelled of liquor and perfume. Both in profuse measures.

'You look so pretty.' I couldn't help but look at her stomach in the tight golden off-shoulder halter dress that she was wearing.

If only she knew.

'It's one of my own designs.'

Liar. I had unsuccessfully tried to fit into the same dress at the Gucci store at the Emporio mall earlier this month. But I let her be, she had graver issues to deal with. Like a strip to piss on and hyperventilate over the next morning.

'Here.' I handed her a dress I had been gifted by some random relative who clearly didn't know that I wasn't bulimic.

'Where's my gift?' she asked Sumer, taking the gift from my hand.

So much for not being greedy. Stop, Tanie, you can't be rude to her. She's a nurturer now. She's crossed over.

Sumer shifted his weight from one foot to the other. 'Ummm.'

Liaka's tight jawline tightened further as she realized he wasn't carrying anything in his hands.

Even I hadn't noticed till now that he had walked in empty-handed. I had a vodka tummy to deal with, in my defence.

Liaka began to walk away.

'Liaka...I—'

'Sumer, stop playing with her.'

Sumer and Liaka both looked at me, confused.

'Just check his pocket, Liaka.'

Liaka instantly got to work while Sumer looked on with surprised eyes.

'This is such a pretty bracelet! Wow, you remembered that I like dolphins,' she said, strapping on the delicate gold bracelet that Mom had gifted me on my birthday last year.

I winked at a visibly shocked Sumer. Despite what he had probably done to Liaka, he was my best friend. I couldn't let him face the embarrassment of walking into his girlfriend's birthday party without a gift. And obviously he would have to reimburse me, in whatever way I liked.

'C'mon.' She dragged Sumer away so that she could show off her boyfriend and the bracelet to her friends.

I went to the bar, got myself a drink and looked around. She had called quite a few people. Some recognizable faces from the house party last year, others not. Suddenly, I felt two muscular arms encircle my waist.

'Hi, I've been observing you, standing all by yourself. Your boyfriend must be a prick to leave you alone for some stupid family wedding.'

I turned around. 'Kabir.' I hugged him.

'I thought we were going to do the role-play bit again…'

His words, hot breaths on the nape of my neck. Such a turn-on.

'Kabir!' Sumer broke the moment and our embrace with an enthusiasm that only came to him once he started mixing his alcohol. I saw the whisky glass in his hand.

He gave Kabir a tight long hug. Like they were two drunken buddies, meeting at a school reunion after years.

'I'm certainly not Liaka, Sumer.' Kabir freed himself from Sumer's grip.

Sumer grinned and drank from his glass again.

'Happy birthday, cousin sister. I hope you like it.'

'WOW,' Liaka and I gasped at the same time.

'Thanks, Kabir! I've been hounding those buggers at Emporio for this limited-edition Louis Vuitton bag for so long!'

'When I was in Paris in the summer, I saw the bag and the first person I thought of was you…look at the pattern and the colour tones…it's so chic.'

That stung. Kabir didn't get me a Louis Vuitton bag from Europe. He did get me stuff from Chanel and Gucci, though. Deciding not to be so greedy, I brushed it off as a brother-sister moment.

'Wow Kabir, for someone so macho, you do have quite an eye for fashion and handbags.' The sarcasm from Sumer came out of the blue.

Kabir's smile died instantly.

I shot Sumer a dirty look.

'That's too much sober conversation for my birthday. Everyone, shots, now!' Liaka diffused the situation and dragged everyone to the bar.

At the bar, as Kabir and Liaka got busy with her friends, I dug my nails into Sumer.

'Fucker.'

'I can't hear you,' he said, taking advantage of the loud music.

Kabir came back with a tray of shots. Liaka joined us and we exhausted the tray in no time. Shot after shot. Lime after lime. Salt after salt. Beat after beat.

Drunk, we all hit the dance floor. And tripped on the music. Coupling for some songs. Huddling together in a tight group of four for others.

Sporadically, Liaka and I took our bladder and touch-up breaks, while Sumer and Kabir continued to drink outside. After one such touch-up break, we went back to the boys. They were laughing hysterically at some joke. Kabir's arm was slung around Sumer's shoulders. Sumer was pumping his fist into Kabir's chest. Like perfect buddies. This was everything I had wanted from day one. I said a quick drunk prayer, thanking God for the wonder of alcohol and time.

'Ladies...' Kabir slurred, on seeing us. I had never seen him so drunk and happy around Sumer.

'Ladies...' Sumer tried to imitate him.

And both of them laughed again. This bonding. So homo. So cute.

'Liaka...we're also here...stop ignoring us!' one of her friends shouted out to her from the dance floor.

As soon as Liaka left, Sumer spoke. 'Okay, you sick couple, make out, while I go to my car.'

'Whhyy?' I slurred. The shots had done their magic. The night was turning out to be by far the best night, ever.

'Beeecaaause, Tan Tan...' He pulled me close. 'I did not forget to get Liaka a gift, I was just waiting for,' he hiccupped, 'the right time.'

'Aye! That's my girlfriend you're talking to.'

I broke free. Immediately.

'Aye! That's my best friend I'm talking to.'

Both the guys started laughing again. I relaxed.

Sumer pulled me to him again and whispered into my ear, 'Tanie, I'm sorry for the whole Liaka bit... I swear, I'll rectify it tomorrow morning...I'm sure we're not in trouble... You'll thank me instead for the surprise I have planned for her.'

'I hope so, Sumer. I hope everything goes fine.'

He kissed me on the cheek and then grinned at Kabir, who faked a punch at him.

'I'll be back.' Sumer left.

Kabir and I started to dance again.

'Tanie, I need to take this caalll...it's my baby sisterrr...you know how much I luuuve her, right?' Kabir sang, a few minutes later.

'Yes, Kabir. I do. Even my feet hurt now.'

'I'll come back and massage them for you. I'll work my magic,' he said, rubbing his leg against mine seductively.

'GO.' I pushed him away.

He went out and I sat on a sofa. Tired, drunk and happy.

I had just taken off my heels and was massaging my feet when my phone buzzed. It was a message from Sumer:

'Tanie, don't question, don't ask anything. Just come out to the parking lot. Find my car. And get Liaka with you. Quickly and yes, I'm in the car...it's a big surprise!'

I was just done reading his message when he messaged again. *'Quick!!!!!'*

Instantly I sprang up from the sofa, heels in my hand, searched for Liaka and pulled her away from the floor.

'Whhaaa...Tanie! Come dance...'

'Something's happened to Sumer outside...we need to rush...he's in his car.'

She darted, faster than me.

So much love. Touchwood.

We reached the parking lot. Drunk. In short dresses. And started to look for Sumer's car.

'There.' Liaka finally spotted it. In a dark corner.

She rushed to the car and I tried to keep up with her, not wanting to miss the big moment. The alcohol threatening to make me trip.

She opened the door of his car. And...

SURPRISE!

'WHAT THE FUCK?' Kabir shrieked.

I froze at what I saw. So did Liaka.

'Thank God, I was just about to get raped,' Sumer said, pushing Kabir, who was sitting on the passenger seat, away from his crotch.

'K...a...b...i...r.' It took a mammoth effort to get the syllables to form a word.

'Tanie...this isn't what it looks like.' Kabir pulled up his pants.

A tent in his boxers. His shirt unbuttoned. Sumer got out of the car. Quickly.

What the fuck was happening? My head throbbed. Eyes hurt. Head started to pump overtime. Big time.

'Tanie!' Sumer shook me.

I returned to the fucked-up reality of life.

'This guy has been lying to you.'

He was okay with not having sex. He knew his belts and shoes. He opened doors. He smelt nice. He never complained when I went out shopping with him. He loved to work out with his trainer. He was a perfect boy. He was gay.

My stomach churned. I took a deep breath and tried hard to compose myself.

Liaka stood there, as confused as I was.

In the meantime, Kabir got out of the car. All dressed up again.

'What the fuck, Sumer? You brought me here...Tanie... Tanie...'

'Don't you dare touch her, you lying scumbag!' Sumer pushed him away.

'Listen Sumer...you're just drunk...you asked me to show you...my tattoo...that's why I was taking off my shirt... What the fuck are you trying to do?'

'Oh yeah? And your pants? I wanted to see your boxers as well?'

'Liaka...your boyfriend is mad...he's trying to...he loves Tanie...that's why he's doing all of this. Jeal—' He couldn't complete his sentence.

Sumer landed a huge-ass punch on Kabir's face. He fell to the ground.

'Tanie.' He looked at me again.

I blinked hard; something salty was stinging my eyes.

Sumer played a voice note on his mobile. The recording echoed claustrophobically despite the space around us.

'You know what, Sumer, I've always told Tanie that you're a good guy. I'm so glad you think the same about me...now.'

'It's okay, man.'

'So tell me, Sumer...'

'Haha, Kabir...why do you have your hand on my thigh?'

'Just.'

'Ummm...'

'Sumer...so Liaka's been telling me you like to do her hard and rough.'

'Kabir…dude…are we really discussing sex, now?'

'Hahaha…says the guy who called me outside. C'mon, you know Tanie doesn't have to know…'

'And Liaka?'

'Hahahahaha…I'm sure if you got me drunk…called me outside…you know…she doesn't have to know either, right?'

'I have no idea what you're talking about, Kabir.'

'Oh c'mon, you sure do, Sumer.'

'Why are you opening your shirt?'

'Why aren't you stopping me then? It's okay…this won't change you…I'm sure you're into girls…but you also know that when a guy gets on his knees, he means business… God…how drunk am I? I'm saying shit…'

'I think we should go.'

'Should we?'

'HEY! Wear your pants, man! You're drunk.'

'So are you.'

'Damn…'

'Hey, who are you messaging?'

'Liaka, so that she doesn't come outside looking for me.'

'Haha…you know, Liaka knew all along.'

'WHAT?'

'That I'm…you know…into this…and I find her boyfriend hot. In fact, I found you cute the moment I saw you in the car, when we raced…then when I saw you at her house party, I was like, fuck dude! How I wish he's into men. But then Liaka told me you're the same guy she was dating earlier, and you know the bitch she is, she has still been talking about how much this can do…'

'Hey man, control your hands.'

'Ooh…he's playing hard to get now. I like that. Question is, how hard are you, otherwise?'

'Uhm…Kabir…I'm really drunk, man. Don't do this…let's just go inside…Tanie…'

'Hahaha Tanie...hahahahah...now you remember your best friend. Don't worry, she's my girlfriend too.'

'FUCKER, you're playing with her heart.'

'Am I now? Okay then, let's forget Tanie and pretend this never happened, okay? After it happens once though...hahahah.'

'I can't lie to Tanie, she's my best friend.'

'She won't know, man, she's too dumb to know anything. She didn't even guess that Liaka set me up with her to get back at her...and then she turned out to be the perfect alibi...you know, she doesn't want sex and making out is mechanical...and the world won't ever doubt me...she's hot.'

Silence.

'Oops...did I say something I shouldn't have... Hahahah...I'm so stoned...that was such a good joint.'

'You had it all...'

'Sorry... Okay now, we need to be quick about this...'

The recording ended.

'Sumer, I...'

Sumer threw a murderous look at Liaka. She zipped it up immediately.

'Tanie, in the evening, what I told you about Liaka...that night, when we hooked up, she went to the washroom, leaving her phone with me as I called for pizza and that's when this fucker messaged. Something about my size...and I freaked out, went to their chat history and it all came out. That's what I was trying to tell you earlier at home also...she's not pregnant.'

'What?' Liaka shrieked.

'Though I regret using a condom now.' Sumer shut her up.

'Tanie.' Kabir had stood up.

I should have cried. I should have howled. I should have scratched Liaka's face. I should have hugged Sumer. I should have done everything but...

'Kabir…' I stretched out my arms.

He walked forward. And just when he was within hugging distance, I made full use of my heels and they connected where it hurt him the most. He doubled up in pain and fell to the ground again.

Liaka squealed. I turned towards her, but Sumer stopped me. He walked up to Liaka.

'Liaka…this for making me fall for you all over again. And I mean it. I'll be honest about this.' His eyes turned moist. 'I fell for you.'

The dam broke. Not from his eyes. But his mouth. A bitch with puke on her. A liar with swollen balls.

Two best friends with moist eyes, slurry tongues and broken hearts walked to the car.

We got in. Sumer threw the keys at me. He was too drunk to drive. Not that I felt any more sober. But reason had failed the night. So had words.

We drove to Sumer's house in a cloud of alcohol and confusion. Trying our best to keep realization at bay.

We entered his house and collapsed onto the couch. Two silent minutes later Sumer got up, staggered to his room and came back with a bottle of cough syrup. I looked at it, then at him as he crashed back on the couch. I knew he meant that there was no alcohol left to handle the pain. I also knew cough syrup wasn't exactly the best bet. But both of us were too tired to articulate emotion and filter it through logic.

We sat there, single again, yet together, not sharing a word of our pain.

After what seemed like an eternity, he suddenly whispered, quite unemotionally, 'Tanie, my ass feels numb.'

I replied in the same drained-out tone, 'Sumer, my heart feels numb.'

A tear rolled down his cheek.

'I fell for a slut.'
I wiped it for him.
'I fell for a gay guy.'
'I'm so stupid.'
'I'm so stupid.' A sudden realization hit me. 'He said he was stoned…that means he smoked up as well.'
'Yes.'
'Did you also?'
Sumer didn't say anything.
'DID YOU ALSO SMOKE UP?'
'You know I wouldn't touch drugs, or a cigarette, for that matter, Tanie. I know how much you hate it.'
We fell silent again. Sitting lifelessly.
Five minutes later, he spoke again. 'She discussed my size with him.'
I stirred. And processed what he had said. 'At least she cared about it, Sumer. He didn't care about my body.'
He turned around and spoke with intention. 'I do.'
'Huh?'
'Let's have sex?' He held me by my shoulders and shook me.
'Are you crazy?' I pushed him back.
'Wait…' He took off his pants.
I closed my eyes. 'Why are you taking off your pants? You're drunk,' I shouted. Too tired to entertain more drama.
'Look…open your eyes…I'm not drunk,' he slurred.
'NO!'
'Open them.'
I tried to resist but failed. He clasped my hand and took it towards his thigh. Violently.
'Leave my hand!' I struggled. But he overpowered me.
'See.' He placed my hand on his thigh. Just where his boxers ended.
'OH!' I gasped.

There was something tattooed on his thigh. An anchor with a thread of words around it.

Sumer read it out in the faintest of whispers, 'Sumer and Liaka.'

I choked.

He looked at me. 'I didn't forget her birthday gift, Tanie. I remembered it, even as I got this, last week. Before I saw the messages on her mobile.'

You know that moment when the anaesthesia wears off and you hurt like a bitch? It had arrived.

Sumer burst out crying. I hugged him. His hands started to shiver. Uncontrollably. He tried to break the embrace.

'I'll just be back. Need to go to my room.'

I didn't let him leave. Crying myself, my fingers entwined with his restless fingers.

'Sumer, are you okay?' I asked him after a while.

His hand hadn't stopped trembling. He broke the embrace successfully now and got up swiftly. 'I'll be back in five. Don't follow. Just five, please.' He dashed to his room.

And I understood that he just wanted to be.

I continued to sit on the couch, thinking to myself, why wasn't I crying as much as Sumer? Despite the similar situation. Sumer came back and answered the question for me. As if he understood what I was thinking.

'You know what, Tanie?' he said hugging me while lying on my lap.

'Hmmm?'

'You loved the idea of Kabir more than Kabir himself. While I loved Liaka, when I thought I loved the idea of loving her.'

I looked at him. He had stopped crying. And his red eyes spoke of the ordeal and the wisdom of what he had just said.

'I can't believe you're giving me relationship advice now.'

We smiled weakly and fell into a comfortable silence. Only for it to be broken by him again.

'Damn…you look so inviting from this position.'

We laughed. Hysterically. I ran my hands over his hair. And looked at my bare wrist.

'That bitch got my bracelet for no reason.'

'Says who? It's in my pocket. I slinked it off her hand while we were dancing.'

We laughed again, till our lungs hurt as much as our hearts did, despite the laughter.

We eventually got up and walked to Sumer's room.

'I could do with some cuddling.'

'So could I.'

We crashed on the bed.

Moments before we passed out, Sumer murmured, 'Tanie.'

'Hmmm.'

'I'm glad we never dated. This feels so much better. Much warmer.'

'Go to sleep, Sumer.'

'Yeah.'

We spooned. As asexually as it could get. Some thirty minutes later, we both still lay awake.

'Sumer.'

'Hmmm.'

'What's that I feel on my leg?'

'Oops, sorry.'

'Yuck.' I pushed him away. Turned to the other side.

And we lay there, single, yet together. Sharing a blanket. The warmth beyond it. And a friendship that only both of us could understand. And no words in the world could define.

'I love you, Tan Tan.'

'I love you, Summu.'

He smiled. She smiled. Problem solved.

We're often told to choose the right over the wrong. Tread the familiar path. Play it by the book. Be safe. And guarded. For everything to be rosy and bright.

I disagree.

I'm telling you, experience the wrong, make that mistake, cry over it and when you're done, you'll see the right with clear eyes.

Sumer and I had both made our mistakes. And learnt. Yes, we did go through the entire routine of heartache. But time, conversation, cheesy movies, a lot of beer and the sheer pleasure of knowing that your best friend is as fucked up as you are, saw us through. Kabir and Liaka knew very well that they couldn't try and fuck with us any more. We had enough proof to fuck them in the ass. Now that we knew both of them enjoyed it. As the months went by and the year ended, Kabir and Liaka became a joke rather than a reason to cry over. Like an old book that lies dusty on the shelf of your life. Not to be thrown, neither to be visited.

2015 started. Sumer got Liaka's name lasered into a dark line. We left our teens. Biologically only. Sumer got back to his old ways of trying his best to contract an STD before he turned twenty-one while I chose to stay single and happy at that. That semester, he even studied for his exams. Almost behaving like an engineer. That scared me, but I made peace with it. Realizing that the best way to move forward is by making the present busy, I got heavily involved in college activities.

Finally, in May, the second year of college ended and we drove back home, our friendship stronger than ever before.

In June, the school gang met again. Had the same fun. Made the same promises. And departed with the same lies. July happened and Sumer's father returned, days before the results. The results came out. I did pretty well. But it was Sumer who surprised everyone. Vikram uncle could also have smooched him that day. He was that happy.

Sumer got a new 5-D video camera out of him in the bargain. His latent dream still residing at the edges.

Life was just about perfect. We were counting the days when we would go back to Delhi and live it up all over again.

And then his father got a hard-on again. And decided to fuck everything up. Just that it turned out to be strike three.

Final and out.

26 July 2015
7.00 p.m.

'I will cut your balls,' I shouted into the phone. I was at the 'other' parking lot of Sukhna Lake in Chandigarh. The one near its dam, away from commercial activity. People. And the police. Surrounded by wilderness. Used religiously only by joggers and lovers with cars. For exercise. Of different kinds. Inside or outside the car.

'Hello to you too, Tanie.'

'I can't believe you ditched jogging with me for some skank who could blow you.'

'Tanie, breathe first.'

I reluctantly followed his instructions.

'Good,' he continued. 'Now I have no idea what you are talking about, unless you went drinking instead of jogging.'

'How about you shut up, Sumer? If I want, I can come and embarrass you right now.'

'Come. I'm in my room, in my boxers, playing with my balls.'

'You're lying.'

'I seriously don't have any idea what you're talking about… here, Santu just came into my room…I'm at home…Santu, say "I love you" to Tanie didi.'

'Hellu...' his servant began.
'Say it, Santu...'
'Hellu, Tanie didi...I love you.'
Sumer came back on the phone and laughed.
'Okay, now stop finding reasons to call me. Come quickly, Stuti called, we are going for a movie.'

I cut the call absent-mindedly. If Sumer actually was home, then...

7.20 p.m.

Conversation between Sumer and I.

'Sumer, stay home. Cancel the movie plan with Stuti. And don't leave your house. I'm coming over.'
'What happened? Why are you panting?'
'Nothing, just don't leave.'
'Attention whore.'
'Where's your mom?'
'Why?'
'Where's your mom?'
'Home. In her room.'
'Cancel the plan. And don't leave.'
'Tanie are you sure everything is okay...hello? Hello, Tanie?'

7.39 p.m.

'Yellow.' Sumer was typing something into his phone as he opened the door and casually greeted me.

On not hearing a reply, he looked up and realized that I was shaking. And the sweat was hardly from the jog.

'Tanie, are you okay?' He guided me inside, made me sit on the sofa and got me water.

I drank it with shaky hands.

'Tanie, what happened?' he asked, genuinely concerned.

I looked at him. Then at the blow-up of his family photo behind him. All smiles.

'Tanie.' Sumer snapped his fingers in front of my eyes.

'Huh.'

'You're scaring me now.' The worry in his voice was evident.

I took a deep breath. If I had started this, I had to put an end to it also. 'Sumer, promise me, whatever I tell you right now, you won't do anything that will hurt anyone you love.'

'Are we making out in front of our parents?' He smiled weakly.

I did not react.

'Okay. Enough with the suspense. I promise.'

I took a deep breath.

'Call Aunty, I need to talk to you both.'

Aunty came and sat on the sofa next to Sumer after he called out to her.

Both of them looked at me, confused.

I swallowed a dry lump, yet couldn't muster the courage to speak. My heart threatened to jump out of my body. It was beating that fast. I looked at Aunty and then finally Sumer. As much as I hated what I was going to do, I knew I needed to do it right here, right now, for my best friend and the most important person in his life.

I took out my mobile from my pocket, clutched Sumer's hand with the other hand and cleared my throat. 'I don't know if this is the right way to do it, but I need to show both of you this.'

The video started to play.

A muddled recording. In the almost dark evening. Sumer's car. The camera zoomed in, pixelating the clarity. A vaguely familiar silhouette. A man. With another curvy silhouette, with long hair. The two silhouettes colliding. And the lines of reality becoming as blurred as the equally blurred video.

The fifteen-odd-second video ended after what seemed like a lifetime. Not a face in the room had colour in it. No sound made its presence felt. Aarti aunty was too shocked to react. Sumer's nails dug into my hand. Even as I heard his breathing increase rapidly. A hot tear rolled down his cheek.

And just then Uncle walked in.

'Sumer...' I gasped, as he freed his hand and dashed towards his father.

What happened next changed everything.

Sumer pinned Vikram uncle to the ground. Aarti aunty shrieked. I rushed to get Sumer off him. Sumer refused to stop. Despite all my efforts. A mad rage had overtaken him. Another blow.

'YOU FUCKER...THIS ONE IS FOR BREAKING MY MOTHER'S HEART AND CHEATING ON HER.'

Vikram uncle tried his best to throw Sumer off. And failed.

Another blow. This time bloody.

'THIS IS FOR SHATTERING MY DREAM. AND MAKING ME DO ENGINEERING.'

Another blow.

'THIS IS FOR ALL THE BEATINGS I TOOK THINKING YOU'RE ACTUALLY MY FATHER...AND A GOOD MAN.'

Hot tears. Shouts. Growls. Shrieks.

Vikram uncle tried his best to defend himself. And in one quick move turned the tables and pinned Sumer down.

One blow to him.

'SUMER! NO! UNCLE, STOP!' I shouted at the top of my lungs.

'VIKRAM, STOP!' So did Aunty.

'Vikram, stop, or I'm calling the cops.'

Never Kiss Your Best Friend

Vikram uncle stopped on hearing that. Aarti aunty told me to take Sumer to his room. I tired my best to do so. Sumer refused to budge and looked at his mother. Aarti aunty, through her tears, pleaded to Sumer.

Sumer stomped to his room. I walked after him. He tried to slam the door in my face. I used all my physical strength to make sure he didn't. After a struggle, he finally let go. I walked in and tried to hug him. He pushed me away. I tried again. He pushed me away violently, once more.

'Just leave, Tanie!' His body shivered as brutally as his voice.

I tried to comfort him. He told me to leave again. I ignored him. He hurled a string of abuses at me. I still stood there firmly. He threatened to slap me. I held his hand and asked him to do so. And without even blinking an eye, he did.

The slap was wild.

I fell down on the ground. Shocked. He did not come forward to pick me up. I managed to get up as I fought tears.

'Leave now. I don't want to be with anybody.' There was no remorse in his voice.

I left, slamming the door behind me.

I walked out of the room. And Sumer's life.

That was the last time we saw each other.

Sumer left with his mom for his nani's place in Mumbai the very next day. He texted me to inform me of that from the airport. I had just woken up after a night through which I had hardly slept. I called him as soon as I read his message but he cut my call. And simply sent me an *'I'm sorry for the slap. Hate me forever'* WhatsApp message. Switched off his phone. He did not reply to any of my calls, messages or texts for the entire week. Eventually, word spread. Everyone from the gang asked me about what had happened and what was going to happen.

If only I knew.

College started. But I did not have the energy to go back. I stayed home for another week, always anxiously waiting for Sumer to call or message or even just come online on Facebook. Mom and Dad were at their supportive best throughout this period—not just for me, but for Aarti aunty, Mom's best friend, who had been cheated on.

Because we're mortals and we suck at freezing time, I eventually went back to college.

'Life has to go on, Tanie. He will get back to you, once everything falls into place,' my mom told me as I sat in the train to Delhi.

College started. And I hated it. Sometime in mid-August, Sumer suddenly called me and told me that his mother was getting a divorce. Vikram wanted to reconcile but Aunty had been cheated on enough in her life, in her own words.

The next week, he called me at 4 in the morning. He had dropped out of engineering college for good and once the divorce came through, he would be leaving with his mother for the US. Forever. We talked for a bit but Sumer had changed. Become too distant. Unemotional. And eventually, the call was cut.

I cried a lot during those days. Feeling helpless. Strangely believing it was my fault all of this was happening. I even thought of flying to Mumbai to meet him and messaged Sumer about that. He called me and categorically told me not to come.

'I'll come down to Chandigarh, with Mom, the day she has to appear in court, or I'll meet you in Delhi.'

That phone call sealed the end of us. I knew that he wouldn't meet me. He was lying. His voice said it. The pauses he took. The tone he used. It hurt. To know someone so well that you know when they're making false promises to you, just by hearing their voice.

But somehow I couldn't hate Sumer. He had never got along with his father. Then he found out that Vikram wasn't his biological father. And he gave up his dream for his mother's happiness, which again came from that father's wish to see him become an engineer.

This wasn't a wound. It was an affliction. And it had cut enough to drain away all the emotion Sumer felt.

September ended.

In October, Sumer simply deleted his Facebook account. Just like he had randomly decided to delete me from his life.

He left for the US, sending me one last message, which simply said, *'Goodbye.'*

If only it were so easy.

He didn't bother calling from the US. Neither did he stay in touch with anyone from the gang.

In December, when I went back to Chandigarh, I learnt that Vikram uncle had sold his house and shifted to Gurgaon.

Then on my birthday in March the following year, as I started my first job, I got a 'Happy Birthday' postcard from the US without a name.

I knew who had sent it. And I threw it in the dustbin.

What Sumer and I had shared was special. There was a time when I couldn't live life without him. Then there came a time when he left my life, without informing me. And now, I had chosen a life without him.

All by myself.

Part 3

Regret. And a few choices.

18 April 2020
12.30 p.m.

'Tanie…Tanie…Tanie…'

I stirred.

'Tanie, are you okay?'

I blinked. Trying to fight the faint traces of darkness, yet not wanting to accept the light.

This, the story of my life.

'Tanie?'

Disoriented, I looked at Shruti. She held out a glass of water to me. I drank it silently, without reasoning with my head as to whatever was happening now, or whatever had happened last night.

Shruti took the glass from my hand. 'Are you sure you're okay? What happened? Why haven't you changed? Did you puke in the washbasin?'

Questions. A lot of them. Answers. None.

I just looked back at her blankly.

'Tanie, say something! Weren't you with a friend?'

FRIEND…

And suddenly the realization hit me. Last night. The club. The alcohol. The drive. The singing. The sea. The kiss. The heaviness in my head. The pain in my heart.

Sumer. Him. Me. Us. Whatever that was. From the day we met. To the day we re-met. And the night we separated again.

I cleared my throat to speak. It still felt dry. 'I'm fine, Shruti.' I got up from my bed and fell back almost immediately.

Shruti came and sat with me on the bed. 'Okay, this is officially scary. Were you drugged?' she tried to joke, even though her tone spoke otherwise.

'I'm fine, Shruti. Just a bad night.'

Shruti scrutinized me for a few moments. Then gave up and lit a cigarette. After taking a drag, she offered it to me.

An unlit cigarette harms more than a burnt one. A broken heart hurts less than a heart that's not experienced love. Sumer's voice boomed in my ears.

I refused the smoke, trying to block all the memories of last night. Like it had never happened. We hadn't met. Or relived a lost friendship. And then kissed like lovers.

It just hadn't happened.

'Wow, Tanie says no to a smoke the first thing in the morning. Are you sure you're fine?'

'Yes.' I smiled weakly.

'Cool. I'll go take a shower. Now that you haven't even asked, I had an amazing time last night. He was hot.' Shruti got up and began to walk out.

That's how adult friendships are. Concerned to the point of practicality. But then my childhood friendship hadn't served me better either.

Shruti stopped at the door and turned around. 'By the way, the maid's not coming today, so please clean the mess you made in the—' Her phone buzzed, stopping her from completing whatever she was about to say.

'Why are you calling me, Tanie?'

'Huh?'

'Tanie, you're calling me.' She walked back to the bed and held out the phone to my face.

'I...my phone...must...'

Shruti raised an eyebrow and answered the call, putting it on speaker. 'Hello?' she said cautiously.

'Hi…sorry to bother you on a Sunday, but could I talk to Tanie?' a masculine voice boomed out of the speaker. And its familiarity hurt.

'Umm…hello?' he said again.

'One second.'

It didn't take Shruti an Einstein moment to solve the equation in her head. I had my phone till last night. Then I had met a friend. Next morning, she had found me all fucked up in my room, without my phone. And there was definitely something shitty happening. Something that she wasn't compelled to understand. She threw the phone at me and walked out.

'Hello?' he said.

I cut the call.

Sumer called back again. And I cut his call again. The cycle was repeated a few times, until Shruti shouted from the kitchen, 'Talk to whoever that is, Tanie, he has your phone. And if you don't care about it, I need my phone!'

The phone rang again. And reluctantly I answered the call. 'Speak.'

'Good afternoon to you too, Tan Tan,' he spoke as warmly as he could. Like nothing had happened.

'You have my phone,' I replied in the coldest tone I could muster.

'That I do.'

'Leave it with the guard. You know where I live.'

'No.'

'Huh?'

'I'm not leaving the phone with your guard. Meet me and take it.'

I dug my nails into the pillow. And spoke as maturely as I could. 'Sumer. Just. Leave. The. Phone. With. My. Guard.'

'Tanie. I. Am. Not. Doing. That.' He laughed.

And the urge to boil his balls surged through me. I took a

deep breath and articulated each word firmly and clearly, punctuating it with angry pauses.

'Sumer, leave my phone with the guard. I need it. This isn't school. I work. I need to answer calls. I don't have my nana's inheritance, and even if I did, I wouldn't want to blow it up for a living.'

'Ah. She's hitting below the belt now. I like it. I like it. Tan Tan, it's a Sunday. If anything, you should be thanking me for keeping you away from work. Eight p.m., under your building. See you.'

'I'm not coming anywhere.'

'Cool. See you. And oh, I was just going through your messages. Call your mom and stop being a bad child. It was so easy to guess your password, guess I know you too well.'

'FUCK YOU.'

'That's thoughtful. But please don't shout, I'm sure you're as hungover as I am.' He cut the call.

'Argh!' I was about to throw Shruti's phone when she shouted from the door. She had been standing there since whenever.

'Hey!'

My hand froze mid-air. And I looked at her, my nostrils still flared.

'As I said, you might not need your phone. But I do need mine. Meet him, Tanie. Get your phone. We're too poor to let the heart rule for a change. Let's just accept it.' She smiled and walked out.

'I'm not meeting you, Sumer,' I angrily muttered to myself and slumped back on the bed.

'I'm not meeting you, Sumer. EVER.'

'Damn. I genuinely thought for a moment that you weren't going to come.' Sumer grinned.

He was standing under my building, outside his car. It was 8.45 p.m. He had been waiting there for the last forty-five minutes.

I extended my hand, signalling for my phone. Swiftly, Sumer grabbed my hand and crushed me into a hug. Even in that brief moment, I couldn't help but notice that he still used the same cologne I had made him start using way back in college, after I broke up with Kabir.

'Why do I use the cologne you like, Tanie?'

Because I have to hug you often and you need to smell nice for that.

The memory hit like a bolt of lightning. I pulled back immediately. Out of the memory and his embrace.

I cleared my throat, not meeting his eye. 'My phone.'

'My hug.'

It took a mammoth effort but I managed to meet his eye. 'My phone.'

He smiled. 'Your eyes look so much better without all the make-up. That's how I've always liked my Tanie…real…flawed but real.'

'My phone.'

He stared at me now. Hard. And I reciprocated, with the same intensity.

Silence, I think, is the most underrated sound in the world. Regardless of the fabled abilities of shouts and howls, I'm telling you, silence stabs the hardest.

We stood there for a few moments. Trying to evade the questions, yet not wanting to give up on their answers.

Why had we kissed yesterday? Why had we kissed ten years ago? Why had we separated? Why were we here? Were we just friends then? Had we been too late in realizing what we were?

He finally looked away, fished out my cell phone from his pocket and gave it to me. I took it. And turned around to leave.

'You can walk away. From here. And then out of my life again. Without giving me any explanation. Like how I walked out of your life, five years ago. Like how I fucked it up back then and again, last night. You can do all of that, and hate me from your gut. Or you could have a beer with me. One, for us. Despite all the fuck-ups. Just for us. In the moment, together, with each other, without thought or justification or label as to what we share. Tanie, I LOVE YOU.'

I froze.

I heard him go back to his car, start it and wait.

I could have walked forward. And never looked back. I could have continued to live life as I was living it, in its own strangulating way. In all these years I thought I'd lost shreds of happiness with every failed relationship, with every lost opportunity at work, with every bottle of cheap port wine I downed before sleeping, but after meeting Sumer last night, all over again, I realized that happiness was him. And I had lost it the day he had left.

Global warming. Bad guys. Weight issues. Too much drinking. I could blame the world for all the problems. But the truth was that no matter how hard I tried to avoid it, in all these years, Sumer continued to be the thought I couldn't escape at 3 a.m. He was the first person I would run to if I were drunk, in a roomful of people I loved. I never really hated him, even after he left me five years ago, or last night, with the taste of his lips and a thousand unanswered questions.

I walked to his car and sat inside.

We drove to a liquor shop. Without exchanging even a single word. Sumer got out and bought a six-pack of Coronas. He then drove us to a secluded spot near my building.

He opened two bottles and handed one to me. We began to

sip on our beer. Awkwardly. The silence between us was threatening to explode. Sumer realized that. He took my hand in his. My cold hand burned against the warmth of his clasp. And it felt like home.

'Tanie, you remember when we first kissed, ten years ago?'

I felt my heartbeat increase unreasonably. 'Yes,' I whispered back, not being able to meet his gaze.

Sumer smiled. 'You remember how, after you came back from Singapore…and walked into my room only to find me…'

I smiled and looked at him now. 'Yeah…And then the kidnapping, and finally how we drove to the liquor shop, to talk it out over beer.'

'Nothing's changed, Tanie. Except the fact that one beer feels like a mouth gargle now and you've become prettier and I more hideous. Ten years later, life has come full circle. We're still in a car, drinking beer, trying to avoid discussing a kiss and what we feel for each other. At that time, you chose not to talk to me for three months and this time, I chose not to talk for so many years. I told you I loved you then. You thought you didn't. Today, I'm asking you again, do you love me, Tanie?'

I tried really hard to fight back the tears. But they escaped.

Sumer cupped my face and whispered, 'Somewhere between the choices you made and the decisions I took, we lost our laughter, Tanie. It's time we bring it back. Not as friends. Not as lovers. Undefined by society. Just being us…I said it ten years ago and I'm going to say it again…I love you, Tanie Brar.'

'I love you, Sumer Dhillon.'

We both burped. And then kissed. Softly at first. Then like hungry vultures scavenging on each other. The car shook. Our hearts pumped vigorously. An old couple walking past the car scowled. But we did not stop until we were exhausted with all the making out. We went for round two in my building's lift.

'There are cameras!' I tried to stop him.

'Let's get famous then.' He didn't stop.

Round three happened as soon as Sumer was done saying hello to Shruti. I pulled him into my room. The clothes came off as soon as the light was switched off.

'Do you have a—' I panted.

'Condom? Yes, I've carried one for ten years. I named it after you.'

'Shut up.'

'But now that I think of it, it might have expired.'

And amidst all the passion, we burst out laughing.

We did not have sex that night. We made love. In it's truest form.

After we were done, Sumer lay spooning me. His heart pumping extraordinarily fast against my back.

'Tan Tan...' he whispered in my ear.

'Hmmm.'

'What would you do if I died tomorrow morning?'

I turned and stared at his face. 'Don't say that again.'

We kissed. He suddenly began to cough and did not stop till he used his inhaler. I rubbed his back, scared by the sudden attack. Even though it wasn't as bad as the one he had gotten yesterday.

'But I could,' he said, after he recovered.

'I told you, stop saying that. It's just asthma, Sumer, don't be a drama queen, it's just the pollution. You'll be okay...'

'Haha...yes. I've been exerting myself too much. And all this pressure of performing for you got to me.'

'Idiot.'

We lay down on the bed again. And spooned. In silence.

After a while, Sumer whispered again, 'Tan Tan, you know, even if I die tomorrow morning and this is the last night we're together, I know I'll never die.'

'What?'

'You're going to be a writer, right?'

'I guess.'

'I've read somewhere that if you fall in love with a writer, you can never die.'

I woke up with a start the next morning. Sumer wasn't there in the bed. I frantically wore my T-shirt and walked to the washroom. It was empty. I put on my shorts and walked to the living room. It was empty as well. I saw the clock. It was 7.30 a.m. Shruti was still sleeping in her room.

Confused, I walked back to my room and switched on my cell phone to call him. I was about to dial his number when I saw the wallpaper on my cell phone's screen. Sumer had changed it. Behind the apps and the icons I could see some text. I moved the apps away so that I could see it properly.

'TAN TAN...I KNOW YOU'RE WONDERING WHY I AM NOT WITH YOU RIGHT NOW. SEARCH FOR THE MS DOCUMENT CALLED 'US'.

I smiled into the phone. Sumer was such a hopeless romantic. He must have gone to get breakfast. And left something for me, to remember him. I searched for the document. And began reading it.

And within seconds my smile vanished.

A COCK'S CRY...
Emotional rants of a heterosexual boy

11 April 2010

This feels so weird.

Writing to you. About you. About us. When all I need to do is to simply press '2' on the speed dial of my cell phone. Or flash my laser light from my window to yours. But the truth is, I can't. No matter how hard I try. Not after that kiss. And the painful four months that have followed.

Okay so...

It's 1 a.m. My laptop is heating my crotch, trying its best to make me impotent, but here I am, in my bed, not streaming porn or playing Counter-Strike, but typing out a letter that I will never email you.

Tan Tan, I'll put it as simply as I can. I know me doing this sounds extremely gay, but the bitch of a truth is that I need a vent. A shoulder. An embrace. Some advice. Maybe a loaded burger. And some alcohol. But there's nothing in the fridge. Not even Nutella. And Dad's bar is locked.

I just don't have a choice. There are so many things going on in my mind that I need to spit them out. Listerine or no Listerine.

So here goes.

Firstly, I never got around to asking, how was Singapore? I'm sure it was awesome. Don't mean to be rude, but I think you've gained a little weight in the last four months. You still look pretty though. So pretty, I could write a poem about you. Just that you'd end up laughing at it. Not like I'd mind. You look the prettiest when you laugh from your heart.

And I mean it. As much as the kiss meant to me...

Okay, sorry, I'm digressing again.

I'm sorry. For three things.

I'm really sorry about what happened in my room. If only you had messaged me that you were coming, I would have known better and locked my room, or made sure I didn't indulge in forearm muscle-building at my hormonal best. If only...

Just so you know, Shanti is still scandalized. Her hands were trembling as she served me dinner. The poor woman couldn't even tell Mom how the cold-coffee tray fell in my room. Haha.

Sorry again for going all Crime Patrol *on you. But you have to agree the kidnapping bit was a cool idea. Imagine, we now have a crazy story to share for the rest of our lives! How cool is that? Okay, I can picture you rolling your eyes, if you were to read this. Haha. But yes, thank you for being sporting enough to not kick me in the balls. No wait, didn't you try stabbing me with the butter knife? Anyway. I'll pretend that never happened.*

So that strikes off two apologies.

But the third one is a little complicated.

It's about that conversation we had. You say you see just a best friend in me. You say that if we date, we would eventually end up losing our friendship. You say that I make you feel real and you want it to remain that way. And a relationship would fuck things up. Sooner or later. You say that I don't love you. I'm just in love with the idea of love, because I broke up with Liaka.

But I totally disagree.

And I'm sorry about it.

If I didn't love you, I wouldn't know that you blink your eyes too hard every time you try to make your point in a discussion. If I didn't love you, I wouldn't want to cup your face and play with your hair or sleep in your lap as I take in the Chanel fragrance you pour over your body every day. If I didn't love you, I wouldn't find you cute when you throw a tantrum. If I didn't love you, I wouldn't find a beat in the weird music you listen to. If I didn't love you, I wouldn't watch The Lord of the Rings, *and that's saying a lot for a* Harry Potter *loyalist.*

Tanie, life around you isn't just about the stars and the moon, it's about the universe of happiness.

And I just love you silly.

So if you still think you love Rehaan, despite all that he did to you and after all that I've done for you, and you just want to be best friends, I'm cool with that.

I'm cool with going to sleep, feeling vacant, sad and empty every night.

It's all good.

I'll hide the dark circles. Stifle the yawns. Mask the heart. Numb the pain.

It's all good.

Just continue to smile. And don't ever leave me.

You breathe, I exist.

Okay, I think I just grew a pair of tits right there. Couldn't get cheesier now, could I? But this exercise actually felt good. Maybe I'll need to do this again.

I'm naming this document 'A Cock's Cry'. Fancy, right?

Goodnight, Tanie. I wish I could tell you all of this. But I can't. So stay in the laptop, with me. And my head.

I need to pretend to be just a best friend again tomorrow morning and that'll require some effort, so I'm off.

---

19 June 2010

I was SO pissed today. Googling ways of making one's father understand that his son doesn't want to do engineering, and then I came across this document on my laptop. That two-month-old rant; but fuck it. I'm just going to write again. Especially after what we were about to do in my backyard last evening.

It kind of helped then. It might help now as well.

So Tanie, I'm going to make this really short and simple. This is getting really hard. And I'm trying my best not to snap. But life isn't exactly helping. Vikram's lost the plot, with his whole 'engineering' rut. Sometimes, I think he's not even my father. I mean, c'mon, you can't seriously be like this! And what's with Mom? Otherwise she has a quota of 25,000 words a day to finish and now, she's silent. Of all the times, now! But I'll wriggle out of this. And won't let Vikram have the final laugh. Filmmaking is my scene and I will direct my life, come what may.

Okay, I think I've already told you all of this in person. What I have not and cannot tell you is that despite all this engineering drama in my life, I cannot sleep, thinking about last evening. We were again about to kiss in my backyard. If only we had, perhaps I would have had something to look forward to tomorrow when I take Vikram on, full throttle.

Tanie, this is getting really difficult. Hiding my true feelings from you. And you're doing a bloody good job of being dumb. Congratulations for that.

Okay, tomorrow's conversation with Vikram is frying my mind but I know you're there for me.

If only it was in the way I wanted.

Because you deserve love.

And I deserve you.

4 October 2010

I'm tired. Really tired.

Life is depressing. My own father doesn't understand my dream and my mother has no objection to that, and I'm stuck in non-medical classes with women with more hair on their bodies than me. (No, I'm not counting the hair on their heads.)

I can manage the hormones. Actually I can't but it's okay, I've got ways; what I can't manage is dealing with the reality of not getting to see you as often as I used to. I miss you. I know I have classes all the time. And physics, chemistry and maths control my life now.

I keep on telling myself that it's all for a cause. Two years of Dad believing that I'm living his dream and then it getting shattered with the results of my Board and entrance exams.

I'm doing this to see that shocked expression on his face. I'll shoot it with a camera. And take it to film school with me.

But that's the end and this journey is so difficult.

I'm writing to you today to tell you a few things that I have been thinking about for a while now and I know I'll never be able to say them to your face.

Tanie, every time you hug me and tell me it's all going to be okay in the end, the embrace touches my soul. And I'm not even being cheesy about it. It does. It makes me want to hug you back so tight, take in all the warmth and live in it.

Tanie, every time you complain that I don't give you enough time now, a part of me dies. And it's restored when I buy you a beer and you smile.

I love the emotional blackmail. At least it makes me believe that somewhere deep down, you miss me at a level you yourself haven't discovered.

I'm just waiting for that realization to hit.

And until it does, I need to get back to quantum physics.

---

24 November 2010

This may sound very mean. But I'm kind of happy that your dog's dead. She stank. Was old. Pooped in my room. And often tried to bite me in your absence. I swear. I saw it in her eyes. She did not like me. I didn't either.

We both had the same person to extract love from.

You know what makes me happier about her death? I got to be the shoulder you cried your heart out on. And left imprints of your mucus on. Even if that ended up with me being grounded for bunking my maths tuition, after bumping into Dad, with you, at the DVD store.

I have to admit, watching Marley and Me *to get over your dead dog is such a silly idea.*

But I love you silly, silly.

That's why I've started to love this—if I said all of this to you in person, you would have castrated me. I like this little secret of ours. It has you, without you knowing you're there. Much like our love story.

---

4 August 2011

Wow! I can't believe it has been almost six months since I opened this document. But then again, class twelve has been so mundane. I think we've lost our charm.

Look at us! You and me. Two goddamn good-looking clean disease-free single teenagers, needing love from those who don't want to give it.

Though I know you wouldn't agree with me, knowing that I've hooked up with two girls from the tuitions in the last six months while you've still stuck to the memory of that asshole Rehaan. Here's a little secret. I'm not a player, Tanie, I'm just a seventeen-year-old who hopelessly loves his best friend even as he makes sure he doesn't die of a sperm overproduction inside his body.

But I'm not writing after so long to tell you about my 'nunu'. I'm writing just to let you know that you looked really pretty today. More than you regularly do. I know, for you it was just another day.

But for me, it became an occasion. And I want to celebrate it with you.

Not simply as your best friend.

---

7 December 2012

That's the funny thing about happiness. Different people find it in different things. Some find it in risking their lives for the adrenaline rush of a speeding car. Some find it in the narrow corners of a bookshop as they escape to another world. Some find it in a cold rush of sea breeze as it hits their face on a sticky night. Some find it in the corridors of their mind as it accepts an alternative reality of injections, smoke and pills. Some find it in losing themselves to a tune that completely fills them up.

Today, I think I found my happiness.

Not because you were clearly jealous of Shanaya and my faked closeness to her. Not even because our lips met again on the steps of F Bar. Even as I wanted to frame our lives to that moment.

But because today you actually let go of Rehaan, his memory, his affliction, and it showed in your eyes.

I found happiness in rediscovering that drunk twinkle in your eye, Tanie. I found happiness, for you rediscovered yourself.

And now that tomorrow will truly be a new day, I won't suddenly bombard you with my love for you. In fact, I'm not going to do it till it's the right time.

For I've learnt a lesson, Tanie. We should love not when we're lonely but when we're ready.

I'll wait for you to get ready.

I have a twinkle to take care of till then.

19 May 2013

This is it.

This is the moment that has been resident in my head for the past two years. After I finish writing this, I'm going to go down, walk up to Dad and show him the letter I got from the film school. I've lived his vision for the last two years and realized I just cannot make it mine.

And the film school is the only flight I have to take me to my land of dreams and choices.

I've never hated Vikram so much. He shouldn't have slapped me yesterday when the results came out. But you know what, Tanie, the funny part is that I'm not as pissed with him about the slap as I am with the fact that he slapped me in front of you. He's challenged the man in me. I'm going to walk down as one now.

Thank you, Tanie, for believing in me.

Last night, when we sneaked out to your garden, I realized that no matter what happens in my life, from now on, I always will have your support.

And today, after this conversation, I probably won't be needing this document anymore either. I'll come and tell you.

I love you.

We're starting a new life soon. College. Even if we are in different cities. I want us to be connected. With all the reality. And no burden of hidden feelings.

I love you.

And now is the time I make you realize that you love me as well.

13 July 2013

I'm sorry.

For the last two months. For not being around. For suddenly going to Mumbai to Nana's place. For making you wonder what's happened to me.

I'm sorry.

For being fucked up. The reality is, I'm more fucked up than you think I can ever be. He's not my biological father, Tanie!

He's the man who saved my mother from sinking into a pool of depression after my father left her, with me as his memory.

Tanie, my mother has sacrificed her necessities in life to fulfil my desires. I love her more than I love myself, my dream or even you.

And I can't see her hurting. If engineering is what her husband wants, it's what I'm going to do. I'll hopefully crack a deal with life in the next four years. And I don't want to think about what will happen if nothing works out. But I'm going to do engineering.

Tanie, there's something else that I want you to know.

I was awake when you kissed me in Shiven's washroom last night, at his farewell party. There's a reason why I didn't kiss you back. And I'm sorry for not telling you this. But I'm scared I might lose you, if you come to know. I've lost you once. And I know how it feels to lose your breath. I don't want to be that way again. I'd rather live guilty than lonely. I know I'm being selfish. But I need you with me.

Tanie…in Mumbai, I met Shanaya a couple of times. I was depressed, stressed and lonely. And she told me she had a solution for it. A weak moment is all that it took. I smoked up, Tanie. I did drugs. I hated it initially. Coughed my lungs out as I saw your face flash in front of my eyes. But as the buzz took over, I felt my pain numb, my senses die and it didn't feel right, but wrong was too far to judge, where I'd ventured. It just felt so non-existent. Like nothing mattered. And I was just a speck of reality. And I hate to admit it but I liked this roll of oblivion.

But the next morning when I woke up, I realized that what I did was wrong and promised myself that I wouldn't ever do it again.

For you. For Mom.

But I needed the courage to tell you about my father, so before boarding the flight yesterday, I met Shanaya and smoked another joint with her.

I know you'd hate me if you knew, you kissed me for who I wasn't. And as punishment, I'm not going to tell you about my true feelings till I find the right time to do so. It might take days, we might start college by then. It may trickle to weeks. But I'm okay with the punishment. For you're beautiful. And you deserve beautiful.

Let the lie die.
And we'll be together, forever.

---

3 May 2017

Because the only plans life acts upon are the ones that you don't plan for.

I just read my last entry. It was another universe ago. Don't ask me why I didn't tell you I loved you. Don't ask me why I never came back to this document. Don't ask me where I lost the years. Don't ask me why I am writing after so long. Don't ask me why I cut off from you. Don't ask me why I am remembering you.

Just read on...
Mistakes.
Personal choices gone wrong. Some of them are trivial. You can balm them with simple repeated scratching. Let them get covered in

darkness. And they are gone. Leaving behind a mere scar. Noticeable yet unimportant. Some of them simply need the brush of an eraser. The little eraser dust pellets, slaves to a subsequent sway of the hand. Some of them inspire a little more effort. They can be locked in dark secret boxes within the body. And forgotten. They can be torn from the pages of a notebook, or the chapters of life, and burned. Some of them are relatively stronger. They feed on tears for a while; seduce mercy and die a negotiated, nonetheless subtle death. Some of them are merely materialistic whores. They don't need emotion. They need compensation. They get it. They leave.

But then there are mistakes that are different. Mistakes that alter aims. Strangulate emotions. Enslave life. Freeze logic. Mistakes that you know will harm you but you still want to commit them. Repeatedly. Like a lousy habit without any reason.

Not telling you that I had smoked up, the very first time, was that mistake. Doing it again with Liaka, thinking of it to be just a one-off, was that mistake. Snorting a line of coke with her at her house party, when we both went to the room, leaving you behind, was that mistake. Letting you go out with Kabir and not telling you how I felt about you because I lived with the burden of lying to you about the drugs was that mistake. Bumping into you, stoned and coked, on your first date with him at Social was that mistake. Distancing you from me and getting close to the world of smoke, chemicals, trance music, acid paper, stamps was that mistake. Realizing that I had become a slave bound by invisible chains to the prison of this intoxication was that mistake. Lying to you about the regular weight loss, the constantly red eyes, the jerky mood swings, the snappy moments or irritation that I went through was that mistake. Seeing you fall in love with Kabir and finding my solace in drugs, for I had lost you all over again, was that mistake. Making myself believe that I had fallen for Liaka and the world of drugs she further perpetuated in our relationship was that mistake. Trying my best to refrain from a habit, now mixed in my blood, all by myself and still not asking for your help to rise above the shallowness of the smoke, even as we became best friends again, was that mistake.

Slapping you in my room, the evening you exposed Vikram and not feeling apologetic about it, purely because the urge of to introduce an alternate injected, fucked-up world to space out the pain that evening, was that mistake.

Leaving you without an answer, walking out of your life, distancing myself from you as I plunged further into darkness, as I tried coping with what had happened after I left Chandigarh and came to Mumbai with Mom was that mistake.

Not informing you that one day in Mumbai, Mom walked in on me, in my room, when I was doing drugs, was that mistake.

I'm in rehab today. Not like the ones they show in the movies. It's as posh as it can get. But the richness hasn't completely been able to take out the beggar for drugs in me. For the longest time, Tanie, I was averse to sense and emotion. To the fact that I had let down a woman who had already been let down by two men in whom she had placed her trust. I had let down a best friend from whom I hid the biggest flaw of my life.

It's been almost two years since I've seen you. Heard your voice. Seen you cry. Laughed with you. And felt alive.

Today, we did this exercise in one of our classes. And that got me thinking about you and this document that I had written for you, ages back. I restored it from my email.

Tanie, I'm recovering. Maybe I'll never recover fully. But I'm trying.

I know I fucked up big time, Tanie. I lied. I hid. I got screwed.

But didn't you ever notice the change? Didn't you see that I was hurting? Did you never notice the bloodshot eyes? Didn't you ever smell the weed on me? Didn't you see the white granules stuck around my nostrils?

I wish you had. I wish you knew I was flawed. I wish I didn't have to cut you out of my life.

But I did it only because I wanted to save you. From me.

I've stalked you forever. I know you've moved on. But if one day I realize that I have regained the power to become the same Sumer who danced in his Tommy boxers in front of you, the first day we met, I'll come back in your life. And ask for a chance.

But I've told myself that it probably won't happen.

That's the problem with life, Tanie, we don't dream, we desire. And maybe you and I will never be a reality. Again, I don't have many motivations in life. You make me want to find one.

Thanks for making me realize that love can save us all.

---

19 April 2020

Addictions.

I tried weed. I tried hash. I snorted coke. I licked stamp paper. I slammed MD. There were so many addictions I had to battle with in the last few years.

But today I'm out of rehab.

Sitting on the bed, next to you, even as you sleep peacefully.

You don't know how long I've waited for this. Today I'm not happy, I'm content.

And now I know I'd never need to go back to any synthetic addiction.

However, there's this one addiction that I know will kill me for sure. As much as I try to stay away from it, I know it will eventually enter the room, creep into the bed with me, put its arms around my neck and choke me delicately, even as I'd try to struggle.

That addiction is being with you.

Tanie, I don't have asthma. How I wish it was just that. I know now you've already guessed why I have a scar on my chest.

So much smoke, so many chemicals had to fuck the lungs and the body. And so they did. As royally as they could.

Third stage cancer. It's living in the lungs.

If I would have stayed, we would have laughed, celebrated and lived the dream I've had for a decade now. And then soon after, maybe a few months later, or a few years, the dream would have turned into a nightmare.

I've given you enough pain. Not again. I wouldn't want to raise your hopes and kill them one random morning when I wouldn't get up, even as you kissed me.

I've given Mom enough pain. I'm tired of seeing her come into my room, hiding all those tears, day after day, tending to me, killing her own life, even as she lives.

She didn't deserve this.

You shouldn't have to go through this.

But I know I deserve what I'm going to do soon.

Day before yesterday, I'd got another attack. It was pretty bad.

The chemo is working sporadically. The medicines have their own mood swings. I was tired of trudging along. Of giving so much pain to people around me. Despite the medicines, every day a part of me continues to die, and I'm tired of giving everyone false hope.

You did not accidentally bump into me in the club. I knew from Shruti's Facebook status (told you I'd been stalking you!) that you were going to going to the club that night.

I wanted to end this.

But not before knowing the answer to the question that has haunted me all my life.

Do you love me or not?

After kissing you two nights ago, I grew weak. I wanted to live again. Your breath gave me the hope of life, but then common sense took centre stage and I knew I couldn't be selfish and make you go through the grind that Mom has been through.

I couldn't handle more guilt.

I wouldn't have come and met you if whatever the forces may be hadn't conspired and you hadn't left your phone in my car.

I promised myself I'd only meet you one more time. And I saw this as a sign.

I took Mom out for lunch last afternoon. I saw her smile after a long time. Then I gave her a nice foot massage at home and she slept off. We didn't talk much but she kept looking at me fondly and smiling.

Tell her I'm sorry for what I became. Let her know, I kissed her on her forehead while she was asleep, as I left the house last evening. Between you and me, I think she'll rediscover life once she's done with the burden of taking care of a sick child. Please help her do so, if she refuses. I know you will. You would want to see the over-enthusastic Aarti aunty, who never had a dull moment, back.

You love me, Tanie. And I love you.

And that is exactly why I'm doing this.

I can't raise your hopes. And then enslave them to regular rounds to the hospital. And maybe there wouldn't be the need for it. Maybe we'd have a junior Sumer. And then one day, he'd not have a senior Sumer.

You told me you love me, and gave me the happiest memory of my life.

By the time you finish reading this, I'll be gone. Forever.

Thank you, Tan Tan, for gifting me a lifetime in the life I've chosen.

I'm going a happy man. I'll be happier if you find your calling in life. Stop smoking, get a grip, find love again and fall in it. Smile, cry and feel from within. Most importantly,

Become an author. Fulfil your dream. Publish your book.

For you know, someone once told me, if you fall in love with a writer, you never die.

Epilogue

*One year later.
19 April 2021
Chandigarh*

'My best friend died. But he lived on. For when you fall in love with a writer, you never die.'

I shut the book and ran my fingers across its cover. *He smiled. She smiled. Problem solved.* A national bestseller. There was pin-drop silence in the bookshop. The crowd, which was bigger than the store's capacity, stood entranced.

And then the applause erupted. I looked at the crowd and smiled from behind my podium. In the first row sat his mom, my parents, Megha, Stuti and Shiven. The mother who wanted to celebrate the best son ever. The old friends who knew that they wouldn't ever find another like him.

And *I*.

A tear rolled down my cheek but I let it be. I knew he was watching and laughing over it.

Exactly a year ago, on this very day, I had lost Sumer. The cops had found his body in his car, parked on the highway. With a razor by the side of his lifeless wrist.

'Ma'am…please come for the book signing,' the bookstore's manager whispered in my ear and I complied.

The queue was unending. And with every signature that I offered, I felt Sumer's presence even more.

I hadn't been able to save him that day. But he had saved me. And my life. Even in death, he had given me a direction and a motivation to live.

Sumer wasn't a best friend to me. Nor was he a lover. He was much more than that. Way beyond anything the dictionary could offer to describe our relationship. He was life to me. And despite trying my best to continue living it, the feeling of him not being here with me made me feel sad, all too suddenly.

Just as I was about to get up, after signing the last book, I saw another book being placed on my table. I didn't look up at the person, just then.

I opened the book. 'For whom shall I sign it?'

'Aaryan Dhillon.'

I froze. And looked up. That face. That voice. It hadn''t changed much. Despite the decade.

'Aaryan,' I gasped. 'Where's Boza?' The words escaped instantly.

He just smiled weakly.

'In my heart. She's been there for ten years.'

'Aaryan, would you like to hear a story? It's about this guy called Sumer I think you know him.'

Aaryan smiled.

'Only if you hear mine as well. It's about a girl called Boza. I think you know her.'

'Coffee?'

'Coffee it is.'

He smiled there. She smiled here. Problem solved.

Acknowledgements

Life's pretty good. I still have bad hangovers and a maid who bunks work regularly but then there's a new book coming out—the much-awaited sequel to *Just Friends*!

I'm really sorry that I've kept a lot of you waiting, but with all the TV shows happening, juggling them with college and the social pressures of being young and having a life, I ended up skipping a few deadlines. But that's that and the book is here. So here's a big shout-out to all those who matter, in the journey of following my passion and otherwise:

Mom and Dad, for being so annoyingly supportive of every decision I've taken. I'm not an easy kid and you know that. Mom, you're beautiful and I will forever be a proud mamma's boy.

All the family and friends across my little universe, thank you for keeping me going at all times. I'm not a great writer, I'm just a mumbling kid with a lot of crazy stories to share. And they come from you people.

All the readers and those who watch my TV shows, trust me, without you people, I'd practically be nothing. You guys are the best and I love talking to you people online. Come, group hug!

My producers, for getting me to write a TV show at twenty! Super cool stuff.

St John's High School, Chandigarh, Bharatiya Vidya Bhavan, Panchkula, and Symbiosis School for Liberal Arts, Pune, thank you for schooling me in lessons that go beyond texts.

I can be pretty annoying. Aparna Kanjhila, thanks for reading all the random stuff I kept on sending you at odd hours in the night. Nandini Sachdev, you too! Karan, Pranjal, Bani, Satvika, Payal, Sanchit, Namita, Durjoy, Manali, Jyotika—the good life comes with great friends.

Now that all the paid names are done with (just kidding) the biggest hug to everyone at Rupa Publications.

Ritu, Amrita and Kapish, you've all been super patient and super supportive. Thank you for not simply killing me for all the delays and skipped deadlines.

And most importantly, I'm just a kid who likes to write. Like many others, who're even better than me. Thank you God, for making sure I get to live a dream, in ink and smiles.